I0549396

Mary Cary
"Frequently Martha"

Kate Langley Bosher

Contents

MARY CARY
"FREQUENTLY MARTHA"

BY

Kate Langley Bosher

TO VIRGINIA

I
AN UNTHANKFUL ORPHAN

My name is Mary Cary. I live in the Yorkburg Female Orphan Asylum. You may think nothing happens in an Orphan Asylum. It does. The orphans are sure enough children, and real much like the kind that have Mothers and Fathers; but though they don't give parties or wear truly Paris clothes, things happen, and that's why I am going to write this story.

To-day I was kept in. Yesterday, too. I don't mind, for I would rather watch the lightning up here than be down in the basement with the others. There are days when I love thunder and lightning. I can't flash and crash, being just Mary Cary; but I'd like to, and when it is done for me it is a relief to my feelings.

The reason I was kept in was this. Yesterday Mr. Gaffney, the one with a sunk eye and cold in his head perpetual, came to talk to us for the benefit of our characters. He thinks it's his duty, and, just naturally loving to talk, he wears us out once a week anyhow. Yesterday, not agreeing with what he said, I wouldn't pretend I did, and I was punished prompt, of course.

I don't care for duty-doers, and I tried not to listen to him; but tiresome talk is hard not to hear--it makes you so mad. Hear him I did, and when, after he had ambled on until I thought he really was castor-oil and I had swallowed him, he blew his nose and said:

"You have much, my children, to be thankful for, and for everything you should be thankful. Are you? If so, stand up. Rise, and stand upon your feet."

I didn't rise. All the others did--stood on their feet, just like he asked. None tried their heads. I was the only one that sat, and when he saw me, his sunk eye almost rolled out, and his good eye stared at me in such astonishment that I laughed out loud. I couldn't help it, I truly couldn't.

I'm not thankful for everything, and that's why I didn't stand up. Can you be thankful for toothache, or stomachache, or any kind of ache? You cannot. And not meant to be, either.

The room got awful still, and then presently he said:

"Mary Cary"--his voice was worse than his eye--"Mary Cary, do you mean to say you have not a thankful heart?" And he pointed his finger at me like I was the Jezebel lady come to life.

I didn't answer, thinking it safer, and he asked again:

"Do I understand, Mary Cary"--and by this time he was real red-in-the-face mad--"do I understand you are not thankful for all that comes to you? Do I under-stand aright?"

"Yes, sir, you understand right," I said, getting up this time. "I am not thankful for everything in my life. I'd be much thankfuller to have a Mother and Father on earth than to have them in heaven. And there are a great many other things I would like different." And down I sat, and was kept in for telling the truth.

Miss Bray says it was for impertinence (Miss Bray is the Head Chief of this In-stitution), but I didn't mean to be impertinent. I truly didn't. Speaking facts is apt to make trouble, though--also writing them. To-day Miss Bray kept me in for putting something on the blackboard I forgot to rub out. I wrote it just for my own relief, not thinking about anybody else seeing it. What I wrote was this:

"Some people are crazy all the time; All people are crazy sometimes."

That's why I'm up in the punishment-room to-day, and it only proves that what I wrote is right. It's crazy to let people know you know how queer they are. Miss Bray takes personal everything I do, and when she saw that blackboard, up-stairs she ordered me at once. She loves to punish me, and it's a pleasure I give her often.

I brought my diary with me, and as I can't write when anybody is about, I don't mind being by myself every now and then. Miss Bray don't know this, or my pun-ishment would take some other form.

I just love a diary. You see, its something you can tell things to and not get in trouble. When writing in it I can relieve my feelings by saying what I think, which Miss Katherine says is risky to do to people, and that it's safer to keep your feelings to yourself. People don't really care about them, and there's nothing they get so tired of hearing about. A diary doesn't talk, neither do animals; but a diary under-stands better than animals, and you can call things by their right name in a book which it isn't safe to do out loud, even to a dog.

I know I am not unthankful, and I would much rather have a Father and Moth-er on earth than to have them in heaven, but I guess I should have kept my prefer-ences to myself. Somehow preferences seem to make people mad.

But a Mother and Father in heaven *are* too far away to be truly comforting. I like the people I love to be close to me. I guess that is why, when I was little, I used to hold out my arms at night, hoping my Mother would come and hold me tight. But she never came, and now I know it's no use.

There are a great many things that are no use. One is in telling people what they don't want to know. I found that out almost two years ago, when I wasn't but ten. The way I found out was this.

One morning, it was an awful cold morning, Miss Bray came into the dining-room just as we were taking our seats for breakfast, and she looked so funny that everybody stared, though nobody dared to even smile visible. All the children are afraid of Miss Bray; but at that time I hadn't found out her true self, and, not think-ing of consequences, I jumped up and ran over to her and whispered something in her ear.

"What!" she said. "What did you say?" And she bent her head so as to hear bet-ter.

"You forgot one side of your face when fixing this morning," I said, still whis-pering, not wanting the others to hear. "Only one side is pink--" But I didn't get any further, for she grabbed my hand and almost ran with me out of the room.

"You piece of impertinence!" she said, and her eyes had such sparks in them I knew my judgment-day had come. "You little piece of impertinence! You shall be punished well for this." I was. I didn't mean to be impertinent. I thought she'd like to know. I thought wrong.

I loathe Miss Bray. The very sight of her shoulders in the back gets me mad all over without her saying a word, and everything in me that's wrong comes right forward and speaks out when she and I are together. She thinks she could run this earth better than it's being done, and she walks like she was the Superintendent of most of it. But I could stand that. I could stand her cheeks, and her frizzed front, and a good many other things; but what I can't stand is her passing for being truthful when she isn't. She tells stories, and she knows I know it; and from the day I found it out I have stayed out of her way; and were she the Queen of Europe, Asia, and Africa, and the United States I'd want her to stand out of mine. I truly would.

Her outrageousest story I heard her tell myself. It was over a year ago, and we were in the room where the ladies were having a Board meeting. I had come in to bring some water, and had a waiter full of glasses in my hands, and was just about to put them on the table when I heard Miss Bray tell her Lie.

That's what she did. She Lied!

Those glasses never touched that table. My hands lost their hold, and down they came with a crash. Every one smashed to smithereens, and I standing staring at Miss Bray. The way she told her story was this. The Board deals us out for adoption, and that morning they were discussing a request for Pinkie Moore, and, as usual, Miss Bray didn't want Pinkie to go. You see, Pinkie was very useful. She did a lot of disagreeable things for Miss Bray, and Miss Bray didn't want to lose her. And when Mrs. Roane, who is the only Board lady truly seeing through her, asked, real sharplike, why Pinkie shouldn't go this time, Miss Bray spoke out like she was really grieved.

"I declare, Mrs. Roane," she said--and she twirled her keys round and round her fingers, and twitched the nostril parts of her nose just like a horse--"I declare, Mrs. Roane, I hate to tell you, I really do. But Pinkie Moore wouldn't do for adoption. She has a terrible temper, and she's so slow nobody would keep her. And then, too"--her voice was the Pharisee kind that the Lord must hate worse than all others--"and then, too, I am sorry to say Pinkie is not truthful, and has been caught taking things from the girls. I hope none of you will mention this, as I trust by watching over her to correct these faults. She begs me so not to send her out for adoption, and is so devoted to me that--" And just then she saw me, which she hadn't done before, I being behind Mrs. Armstead, and she stopped like she had been hit.

For a minute I didn't breathe. I didn't. All I did was to stare--stare with mouth open and eyes out; and then it was the glasses went down and I flew into the yard, and there by the pump was Pinkie.

"Oh, Pinkie!" I said. "Oh, Pinkie!" And I caught her round the waist and raced up and down the yard like a wild man from Borneo. "Oh, Pinkie, what do you think?" Poor Pinkie, thinking a mad dog had bit me, tried to make me stop, but stop I wouldn't until there was no more breath. And then we sat down on the woodpile, and I hugged her so hard I almost broke her bones.

First I was so mad I couldn't cry, and then crying so I couldn't speak. But after a while words came, and I said:

"Pinkie Moore, are you devoted to Miss Bray? Are you? I want the truest truth. Are you devoted to her?"

"Devoted to Miss Bray? Devoted!" And poor little Pinkie, who has no more spirit than a poor relation, spoke out for once. "I hate her!" she said. "I hate her worse than prunes; and if somebody would only adopt me, I'd be so thankful I'd choke for joy, except for leaving you." Then she boohoo'd too, and the tears that fell between us looked like we were artesian wells--they certainly did.

But Pinkie didn't know what caused my tears. Mine were mad tears, and not being able to tell her why they came, I had to send her to the house to wash her face. I washed mine at the pump, and then worked off some of my mad by sweeping the yard as hard as I could, wishing all the time Miss Bray was the leaves, and trying to make believe she was. I was full of the things the Bible says went into swine, and I knew there would be trouble for me before the day was out. But there wasn't. Not even for breaking the pump-handle was I punished, and Miss Bray tried so hard to be friendly that at first I did not understand. I do now.

That was my first experience in finding out that some one who looked like a lady on the outside was mean and deceitful on the inside, and it made me tremble all over to find it could be so. Since then I have never pretended to be friends with Miss Bray. As for her, she hates me--hates me because she knows I know what sort of a person she is, a sort I loathe from my heart.

When I first got my diary I thought I was going to write in it every day. I haven't, and that shows I'm no better on resolves than I am on keeping step. I never keep step. Sometimes I've thought I was really something, but I'm not. Nobody much is when you know them too well. It is a good thing for your pride when you keep a diary, specially when you are truthful in it. Each day that you leave out is an evidence of character--poor character--for it shows how careless and put-off-y you are; both of which I am.

But it isn't much in life to be an inmate of a Humane Association, or a Home, or an Asylum, or whatever name you call the place where job-lot charity children live. And that's what I am, an Inmate. Inmates are like malaria and dyspepsia: something nobody wants and every place has. Minerva James says they are like veterans--they die and yet forever live.

Well, anyhow, whenever I used to do wrong, which was pretty constant, I would say to myself it didn't matter, nobody cared. And if I let a chance slip to worry Miss Bray I was sorry for it; but that was before I understood her, and before Miss Katherine came. Since Miss Katherine came I know it's yourself that matters most, not where you live or where you came from, and I'm thinking a little more of Mary Cary than I used to, though in a different way. As for Miss Bray, I truly try at times to forget she's living.

But she's taught me a good deal about Human Nature, Miss Bray has. About the side I didn't know. It's a pity there are things we have to know. I think I will make a special study of Human Nature. I thought once I'd take up Botany in particular, as I love flowers; or Astronomy, so as to find out all about those million worlds in the sky, so superior to earth, and so much larger; but I think, now, I'll settle on Human Nature. Nobody ever knows what it is going to do, which makes it full of surprises, but there's a lot that's real interesting about it. I like it. As for its Bray side, I'll try not to think about it; but if there are puddles, I guess it's well to know where, so as not to step in them. I wish we didn't have to know about puddles and things! I'd so much rather know little and be happy than find out the miserable much some people do.

Anyhow, I won't have to remember all I learn, for Miss Katherine says there are many things it's wise to forget, and whenever I can I'll forget mean things. I'd forget Miss Bray's if she'd tell me she was sorry and cross her heart she'd never do them again. But I don't believe she ever will. God is going to have a hard time with Miss Bray. She's right old to change, and she's set in her ways--bad ways.

II
THE COMING OF MISS KATHERINE

Now, why can't I keep on at a thing like Miss Katherine? Why? Because I'm just Mary Cary, mostly Martha; made of nothing, came from nowhere, and don't know where I'm going, and have no more system in my nature than Miss Bray has charms for gentlemen.

But Miss Katherine--well, there never was and never will be but one Miss Katherine, and there's as much chance of my being like her as there is of my reaching the stars. I'll never be like her, but she's my friend. That's the wonderful part of it. She's my friend. And when you've got a friend like Miss Katherine you've got strength to do anything. To stand anything, too.

The beautiful part of it is that I live with her; that is, she lives in the Asylum, and I sleep in the room with her.

It happened this way. Last summer I didn't want to do anything but sit down. It was the funniest thing, for before that I never did like to sit down if I could stand up, or skip around, or climb, or run, or dance, or jump. I never could walk straight or slow, and I never can keep step.

Well, last summer I didn't want to move, and I couldn't eat, and I didn't even feel like reading. I'd have such queer slipping-away feelings right in my heart that I'd call myself a drop of ink on a blotter that was spreading and spreading and couldn't stop. Sometimes I would think I was sinking down and down, but I really wasn't sinking, for I didn't move. I only felt like I was, and I was afraid to go to sleep at night for fear I would die, and I stayed awake so as to know about it if I did.

And then I began to be afraid of dying, and my heart would beat so I thought it would wear out. But I didn't tell anybody how I felt. I was ashamed of being afraid, and I just told God, because I knew He could understand better than anybody else;

and I asked Him please to hold on to me, I not being able to do much holding myself, and He held. I know it, for I felt it.

You see, Mrs. Blamire--she's Miss Bray's assistant--was away; Miss Bray was busy getting ready to go when Mrs. Blamire came back; and Miss Jones was pickling and preserving. I didn't want to bother her, so I dragged on, and kept my feelings to myself.

The girls were awful good to me. Real many have relations in Yorkburg, and if I'd eaten all the fruit they sent me I'd been a tutti-frutti; but I couldn't eat it. And then one day I began to talk so queer they were frightened, and told Miss Bray, and she sent for the doctor quick. That afternoon they took me to the hospital, and the last thing I saw was little Josie White crying like her heart would break with her arms around a tree.

"Please don't die, Mary Cary, please don't die!" she kept saying over and over, and when they tried to make her go in she bawled worse than ever. I tried to wave my hand.

"I'm not going to die, I'm coming back," I said, and that's all I remember.

I knew they put me in something and drove off, and then I was in a little white bed in a big room with a lot of other little beds in it; and after that I didn't know I was living for three weeks. But I talked just the same. They told me I made speeches by the hour, and read books out loud, and recited poems that had never been printed. But when I stopped and lay like the dead, just breathing, the girls say they heard there were no hopes, and a lot of them just cried and cried. It was awful nice of them, and if they hadn't cut my hair off I would have made a real pretty corpse.

The day I first saw Miss Katherine really good she was standing by my bed, holding my wrist in one hand and her watch in another, and I thought she was an angel and I was in heaven. She was in white, and I took her little white cap for a crown, and I said:

"Are you my Mother?"

She nodded and smiled, but she didn't speak, and I asked again:

"Are you my Mother?"

"Your right-now Mother," she said, and she smiled so delicious I thought of course I was in heaven, and I spoke once more.

"Where's God?"

Then she stooped down and kissed me.

"In your heart and mine," she answered. "But you mustn't talk, not yet. Shut your eyes, and I will sing you to sleep." And I shut them. And I knew I was in heaven, for heaven isn't a place; it's a feeling, and I had it.

And that's how I met Miss Katherine.

Her father and mother are dead, just like mine. Her father was Judge Trent, and his father once owned half the houses in Yorkburg, but lost them some way, and what he didn't lose Judge Trent did after the war.

When her father died Miss Katherine wouldn't live with either of her brothers, or any of her relations, but went to Baltimore to study to be a nurse. After she graduated she didn't come back for three or four years, and she hadn't been back six months when I was taken sick. And now I sing:

"Praise God from whom that sickness flew."

Sing it inside almost all the time.

Miss Katherine don't have to be a nurse. She has a little money. I don't know how much, she never mentioning money before me; but she has some, for I heard Miss Bray and Mrs. Blamire talking one night when they thought I was asleep; and for once I didn't interrupt or let them know I was awake.

I had been punished so often for speaking when I shouldn't that this time I kept quiet, and when they were through I couldn't sleep. I was so excited I stayed awake all night. And from joy--pure joy.

I had only been back from the hospital a week, and was in the room next to Mrs. Blamire's, where the children who are sick stay, when I heard Miss Bray talking to Mrs. Blamire, and at something she said I sat up in bed. Right or wrong, I tried to hear. I did.

They were sitting in front of the fire, and Miss Bray leaned over and cracked the coals.

"Have you heard that Miss Katherine Trent is coming here as a trained nurse?" she said, and she put down the poker, and, folding her arms, began to rock.

"You don't mean it!" said Mrs. Blamire, and her little voice just cackled. "Coming here? To this place? I do declare!" And she drew her chair up closer, being a little deaf.

"That's what she's going to do." Miss Bray took off her spectacles. "The Board can't afford to pay her a salary, but she's offered to come without one, and next week she'll start in."

"Katherine Trent always was queer," she went on, still rocking with all her might. "She can get big prices as a nurse, though she doesn't have to nurse at all, having money enough to live on without working. And why she wants to come to a place like this and fool with fifty-odd children and get no pay for it is beyond my understanding. It's her business, however, not mine, and I'm glad she's coming."

"I do declare!" And Mrs. Blamire clapped her hands like she was getting religion. "My, but I'm glad! Miss Katherine Trent coming here! And next week, you say? I do declare!" And her gladness sounded in her voice. It was a different kind from Miss Bray's. Even in the dark I could tell, for hers was thankfulness for the children. Miss Bray was glad for herself.

That was almost a year ago, and now my hair has come out and curls worse than ever. It's very thick, and it's brown--light brown.

I'm always intending to stand still in front of the glass long enough to see what I do look like, but I'm always in such a hurry I don't have time. I know my eyes are blue, for Miss Katherine said this morning they got bigger and bluer every day, and if I didn't eat more I'd be nothing but eyes. If you don't like a thing, can you eat it? You cannot. That is, in summer you can't. In winter it's a little easier.

I never have understood how Miss Katherine could have come to an Orphan Asylum to live and to eat Orphan Asylum meals when she could have eaten the best in Yorkburg. And Yorkburg's best is the best on earth. Everybody says that who's tried other places, even Miss Webb, who gets right impatient with Yorkburg's slowness and enjoyment of itself.

And Miss Katherine is living here from pure choice. That's what she is doing, and she's made living creatures of us, just like God did when He breathed on Adam and woke him up.

At the hospital she used to ask me all about the Asylum, and, never guessing why, I told her all I knew, except about Miss Bray. Miss Katherine had known the Asylum all her life, but had only been in it twice--just passing it by, not thinking. When I got better and could talk as much as I pleased, she wanted to know how many of us there were, what we did, and how we did it: what we ate, and what kind of underclothes we wore in winter, and how many times a week we bathed all over; when we got up, and what we studied, and how long we sewed each day, and how long we played, and when we went to bed--and all sorts of other things. I wondered why she wanted to know, and when I found out I could have laid right down and died from pure gladness. I didn't, though.

Once I asked her what made her do it, and she laughed and said because she wanted to, and that she was much obliged to me for having found her work for her. But I believe there's some other reason she won't tell.

And why I believe so is that sometimes, when she thinks I am asleep, I see her looking in the fire, and there's something in her face that's never there at any other time. It's a remembrance. I guess most hearts have them if they live long enough. But you'd never think Miss Katherine had one, she's so glad and cheerful and busy all the time. I wonder if it's a sweetheart remembrance? I know three of her beaux; one in Yorkburg and two from away, who have been to see her frequent times; but a beau is different from a sweetheart. I'm sure that look means something secret, and I bet it's a man. Who is he? I don't know. I wish he was dead. I do!

When I first came back from the hospital my little old sticks of legs wouldn't hold me up, and down I would go. But I didn't mind that. I just minded not going to sleep at night. But sleep wouldn't come, and I'd get so wide awake trying to make it that I began to have a teeny bit of fever again, and then it was Miss Katherine asked if she might take me in her room. I was nervous and still needed attention, she said, and--magnificent gloriousness!--I was sent to her room to stay until perfectly well, and I'm here yet. Perfectly well because I am here!

That first night when I got into the little white bed next to her bed, and knew she was going to be there beside me, I couldn't go to sleep right off. I kept wishing I was King David, so I could write a book of gratitudes and psalms and praises, and that was the first night I ever really prayed right. I didn't ask for a thing except for help to be worth it--the trouble she was taking for just little me, a charity child. Just me!

And oh, the difference in her room and the room I had left! She had had it painted and papered herself, for it hadn't been used since kingdom come, and the cobwebs in it would have filled a barrel. It had been a packing-room, and when Miss

Katherine first saw it she just whistled soft and easy; but when she was through, it was just a dream.

It is a big room at the end of the wing, and it has three windows in it: one in the front and one in the back and one opposite the door you come in. And when the paper was put on you felt like you were in a great big garden of roses; pink roses, for they were running all over the walls, and they were so natural I could smell them. I really could.

Miss Katherine brought her own furniture and things, and she put a carpet on the floor, all over, not just strips. And the windows had muslin curtains at them with cretonne curtains just full of pink roses, looped back from the muslin ones; and the couch and the cushions and some chairs were all covered with the same kind of pink roses. And as for the bed, it was too sweet for anybody to lie on--that is, for anybody but Miss Katherine to lie on.

There was a big closet for her clothes, and a writing-desk which had been in the family a hundred years--maybe a thousand. I don't know. And one side of the room was filled with books in shelves which old Peter Sands made and painted white for her. She lets me look at them as much as I want, and says I can read as many as I choose when I am old enough to understand them. She didn't mention any time to begin trying to understand, and so I started at once, and I've read about forty already.

There aren't a great many pictures on Miss Katherine's walls. Just a few besides the portraits of her father and mother, oil paintings. And oh, dear children what are to be, I'm going to have my picture painted as soon as I marry your father, so you can know what I looked like in case I should die without warning. I want you to have it, knowing so well what it means to have nothing that belonged to your mother, I not having anything--not even a strand of hair or a message.

Sometimes I wonder if I ever really did have a Mother, or if the doctor just left me somewhere and nobody wanted me. I must have had one, for Betty Johnson says a baby's bound to. That a father isn't so specially necessary, but you've got to have a Mother. Mine died when I was born. I wonder how that happened when there wasn't anybody in all this great big earth to take care of me except my father, who didn't know how. He died, too, and then I was an Orphan.

This is a strange world, and it's better not to try to understand things.

In the winter time Miss Katherine always has a beautiful crackling fire in her room, and some growing flowers and green things. It was a revelation to the girls, her room was. Not fine, and it didn't cost much, but you felt nicer and kinder the minute you went in it. And it made Mrs. Reagan's grand parlors seem like shining brass and tinkling cymbals. I wonder why?

III
MARY, FREQUENTLY MARTHA

I am going to write a history of my life. The things that happen in this place are the same things, just like our breakfasts, dinners, and suppers. They wouldn't be interesting to hear about, so while waiting for something real exciting to put down, I am going to write my history.

I don't know very much about who I am. I wish my Mother had left a diary about herself, but she didn't. Nobody, not even Miss Katherine, will tell me who I was before I came here, which I did when I was three. I know my nurse brought me, but I can't remember what she looked like, and when she went away without me: I never saw nor heard of her again. I don't even know her name. I thought it was fine to play in a big yard with a lot of children, and I soon stopped crying for my nurse.

I never did see much sense in crying. Everybody was good to me, and not being old enough to know I was a Charity child, and by nature happy, they used to call me Cricket. Sometimes some of them call me that now.

A hundred dozen times I have asked Miss Katherine to tell me something about myself, but in some way she always gets out of it. I know my mother and father are dead, but that's all I do know; and I wouldn't ask Miss Bray if I had to stand alone for ever and ever.

Sometimes I believe Miss Katherine knows something she won't tell me, but since I found out she don't like me to ask her I've stopped. And not being able to ask out what I'd like, I think a lot more, and some nights when I can't go to sleep, it gives me an awful sinking feeling right down in my stomach, to think in all this great big world there isn't a human that's any kin to me.

I might have come from the heavens above or the depths below, only I didn't, and being like other girls in size and shape and feelings, I know I once did have a Mother and Father. But if they had relations they've kept quiet, and it's plain they don't want to know anything about me, never having asked.

It would make me miserable--this aloneness would, if I let it. I won't let it. I have got to look out for Mary Cary, frequently Martha, and when you're miserable you don't get much of anything that's going around. I won't be unhappy. I just won't. I haven't enough other blessings.

But not being able to speak out as much as I would like on some things personal, I got into the habit of talking to my other self, which I named Martha, and which I call my secret sister. Martha is my every-day self, like the Bible Martha who did things, and didn't worry trying to find out what couldn't be found out, specially about why God lets Mothers die.

Mary is my Sunday self who wonders and wonders at everything and asks a million questions inside, and goes along and lets people think she is truly Martha when she knows all the time she isn't. And if I do hold out and write a history of my life, it's going to be a Martha and Mary history; for some days I'm one, some another, and whichever I happen to be is plain to be seen.

When I grow up I am going to marry a million-dollar man, so I can travel around the world and have a house in Paris with twenty bath-rooms in it. And I'm going to have horses and automobiles and a private car and balloons, if they are working all right by that time. I hope they will be, for I want something in which I can soar up and sit and look down on other people.

All my life people have looked down on me, passing me by like I was a Juny bug or a caterpillar, and I don't wonder. I'm merely Mary Cary with fifty-eight more just like me. Blue calico, white dots for winter, white calico, blue dots for summer. Black sailor hats and white sailor hats with blue capes for cold weather, and no fire to dress by, and freezing fingers when it's cold, and no ice-water when it's hot.

Yes, dear Mary, you and I are going to marry a rich man. (Martha is writing to-day.) I will try to love him, but if I can't I will be polite to him and travel alone as much as possible. But I am going to be rich some day. I am. And when I come back to Yorkburg eyes will bulge, for the clothes I am going to wear will make mouths water, they're going to be so grand. Miss Katherine would be ashamed of that and make me ashamed, but this writing is for the relief of feelings.

But there's one thing I'm surer of than I am of being rich, and that is that there are to be no secrets about my children's mother. They are to know all about me I can tell, which won't be much or distinguished, but what there is they're to know. And that's the chief reason I'm going to write my history, so as to remember in case I forget.

Well, now I will begin. I am eleven years and eleven months and three days old. I don't have birthday parties. The Yorkburg Female Orphan Asylum is a large house with a wide hall in the middle, and a wing on one side that makes it look like Major Green, who lost one arm in the war.

There are large grounds around the house, and around the grounds is a high brick wall in front and a wooden fence back and sides. The children and the chickens use the grounds at the back; the front has grass and flowers, and is for company, which is seldom. Sometimes, just because I can't help it, I chase a chicken through the front so as to know how it feels to run in the grass, which it is forbidden to do.

Forbidden things are so much nicer than unforbidden. I love to do them until they're done.

The Asylum is on King Street, almost at the very end, and there isn't much passing, just the Tates and the Gordons and a few others living farther on. The dining-room is in the basement, half below the ground, and on cloudy days the lamps have to be lighted--that is, they used to. Now we have electric lights, and I just love to turn them on. It's such a grand way to get a thing done, just to press a button.

The dining-room has a picture over the mantel of a cow standing in yellow-brown grass, and, though hideous, it's a great comfort. That cow understands our feelings at mealtimes, and we understand hers.

Humane meals are very much like yellow-brown grass, and our clothes are on the same order as our meals. As for our days, if it wasn't for calendars we wouldn't know one from the other, except Sundays, for, unlike the stars mentioned by St. Paul, they differ not.

The rising-bell rings at five o'clock, and all except the very littlest get up and clean up until seven, when we march into the dining-room. At 7.25 we rise at the tap of Miss Bray's bell, and those who have more cleaning up-stairs march out; those who clear the table and wash the dishes stay behind. At 8.30 we march into the school-room, where we have prayers and calisthenics. The calisthenics are fine.

At nine we begin recitations.

We have a teacher who lives in town, Miss Elvira Strother. She's a good teacher. The older girls help teach the little ones, and next year I'm to help.

This Asylum is over ninety (90) years old, but looks much older. There is just money enough to run it, and it hasn't had any paint or improvements in the memory of man, except the electric lights. The town put those in for safety, and don't charge for them.

I wish the town would put in bath-tubs for the same reason. It would make the children much nicer. They just naturally don't like to wash, and one small pitcher of water for two girls don't allow much splashing.

But Yorkburg hasn't any water-works, not being born with them. I mean, water-works not being the fashion when Yorkburg was first begun, nobody has ever thought of putting them in. Mr. Loyall, he's the mayor, says everybody has gotten on very well for over two hundred years without them, and he don't see any use in stirring up the subject. So there'll never be any change until he's dead, and in Yorkburg nobody dies till the last thing.

There wouldn't be any electric lights if the shoe factory hadn't come here. The men who brought it came from New Jersey, and they wanted light, and got it. And Yorkburg was so pleased that it moved a little and made some light for itself; and now everything in town just blazes, even the Asylum.

I used to sleep in No. 4, but I don't sleep there now. It is a big room, and has six windows in it, and in winter we children used to play we were arctic explorers and would search for icebergs. The North Pole was the Reagan's house, half-way down the street, and it might as well have been, for it was as much beyond our reach.

But it was the one thing we were all going to get some day when we married rich. And when we got it, we were going to drive up to the Galt House--that's the Home for Poor and Proud Ladies--and ask for Mrs. Reagan, who was to be in it in the third floor back, and leave her some old clothes with the buttons off, and old magazines. None of us could bear Mrs. Reagan--not a single one.

It is a beautiful house, Mrs. Reagan's is. It has large white pillars in the front and back, and it's got three bath-rooms, and a big tank in the back yard. And it has velvet curtains over the lace ones, and gold furniture and pictures with gold frames a foot wide.

I heard Miss Katherine talking about it to Miss Webb one night. They were laughing about something Miss Katherine said was the most impossible of all, and Miss Webb said it was desecrating for such a stately old house to fall into the hands of such bulgarians. What are bulgarians? I don't know. But they're not ladies.

Mrs. Reagan is not a lady. The way I found it out was this. Miss Jones, she's our housekeeper, sent a message to her one day by Bertha Reed and me about some pickles. Bertha is awful timid, and she didn't know whether or not we ought to go to the front door; but I did, and I told her to come on.

"I don't go to back doors, if I don't know my family history," I said. "I know who I am, and something inside of me tells me where to go." And I pressed the button so hard I thought I'd broken it unintentional.

The man-servant opened the door and looked at us as if weary and surprised, and said nothing.

"Is Mrs. Reagan in?" I asked.

"She is."

That's all he said. He waited. I waited. Then I stepped forward.

"We will come in," I said. "And you go and tell her Mary Cary would like to see her, having a message from Miss Jones." And he was so surprised he moved aside, and in I walked.

I had heard so much about this house that I wasn't going to miss seeing what was in it, if that fool man was rude; so while he was gone to get Mrs. Reagan I counted everything in the front parlor as quick as I could, and told Bertha to count everything in the back.

There were three sofas and two mirrors and nine chairs and six rugs and six tables and two pianos, one little old-fashioned one and a big new one; and three stools and seventeen candlesticks and four pedestals with statuary on them, some broken, all naked; and seven palms and twenty-three pictures and two lamps and five red-plush curtains, three pairs over the lace ones and two at the doors; and as for ornaments, it was a shop. And not one single book.

I am sure I got the things right, for I'd been practising remembering at observation parties, in case I ever got a chance to see inside this house; and I looked hard so I could tell the girls.

Poor Bertha was so frightened she didn't remember anything but the clock and a china cat and an easel and picture, and before I could count Mrs. Reagan came in.

She stopped in the doorway, and had we come from leper-land she couldn't have held herself farther off.

"What are you doing in here?" she asked, and she tried the haughty air--"What are you doing in here?"

"We were waiting for you," I said. "We have a message from Miss Jones."

"Well, another time don't wait in here, and don't come to the front door if you have a message from Miss Jones or Miss Any-body-else. I don't want any pickles this year. Had I wanted any I would have sent her word. You understand? Don't ever come here again in this way!" And she waved us out as if we were flies.

For a minute I looked at her as if she were a Mrs. Jorley's wax-works, and then I made a bow like I make in charades.

"We understand," I said. "And we will not come again. We've heard a good many people in Yorkburg have been once and no more." And I bowed again and walked past her like she was a stage character, which she was, being a pretence and nothing else.

Mad? I tell you, I was Martha for a week, and then I saw, real sudden, how silly I was to let a bulgarian make me mad.

But if I'm ever expected to love anything like that, it will be expecting too much of Mary Cary, mostly Martha, for she isn't an enemy. She's just a make-believe of something she wasn't born into being and don't know how to make her-self. She don't agree with my nature, and if I had a parlor she couldn't come into it either. She could not.

IV
THE STEPPED-ON AND THE STEPPERS

I don't believe I ever have written anything about my first years at this Asylum. I am naturally a wandering person. Well, I was happy. I know I've said that before, but Miss Katherine says that's one of the few things you can say often. I had a kitten, and a chicken which I killed by mistake. I took it to the pump to wash it, and it lost its breath and died. I still put flowers on the place where its grave was.

It was my first to die. I have lost many others since: a cat, and a rabbit, and a rooster called Napoleon because he was so strutty and domineering to his wives. I didn't put up anything to his grave. I didn't think the hens would like it. They just despised him.

Then there were the remains of Rebecca Baker. She was of rags, with button eyes and no teeth, just marks for them; but I loved her very much. I kept her as long as there was anything to hold her by; but after legs and arms went, and the back of her head got so thin from lack of sawdust that she had neuralgia all the time, I found her dead one morning, and buried her at once.

I loved Rebecca Baker: not for looks, but for comfort. I could talk to her without fear of her telling. She always knew how hungry I was, and how I hated oatmeal without sugar, and she never talked back.

During the years from three to nine I lived just mechanical, except on the inside. I got up to a bell and cleaned to a bell, and sat down to eat to a bell; rose to a bell, went to school to a bell, came out to a bell, worked to a bell, sewed to a bell, played to a bell, said my prayers to a bell, got in bed to a bell, and the next day and every day did the same thing over to the same old bell.

But when I marry my children's father there are to be no bells in the house we live in. Only buttons, with no particular time to be pressed.

We go to church to a bell, too; that, is to Sunday-school. We always go to St. John's Sunday-school--Episcopal. The man who left this place put it in his will that we had to, but we go to all the other churches. Episcopal the first Sunday, Methodist the second, Presbyterian the third, and Baptist the fourth, and when we get through we begin all over again.

We go to church like we do everything else, two by two. Start at a tap of that same old bell, and march along like wooden figures wound up; and the people who see us don't think we are really truly children or like theirs, except in shape inside. They think we just love our hideous clothes, and that we ought to be thankful for molasses and bread-and-milk every night in the week but one, and if we're not, we're wicked. Rich people think queer things.

Sundays at the Humane are terribly religious.

They begin early and last until after supper, and if anybody is sorry when Sunday is over, it's never been mentioned out loud. We have prayers and Bible-reading before breakfast every day, but on Sundays longer. Then we go to Sunday-school, where some of the children stare at us like we were foreign heathen who have come to get saved. Some nudge each other and laugh. But real many are nice and sweet, and I just love that little Minnie Dawes, who sits in front of me. She wears the prettiest hats in Yorkburg, and I get lots of ideas from them. I trim hats in my mind all the time Miss Sallie is talking--Miss Sallie is our teacher.

She is a good lady, Miss Sallie Ray is. Her chief occupation is religion, and as for going to church, it's the true joy of her life. She's in love with Mr. Benson, the Superintendent, and very regular at all the services. So is he.

But for teaching children Miss Sallie wasn't meant. She really wasn't. She never surely knows the lesson herself, and it was such fun asking her all sorts of questions just to see her flounder round for answers that I used to pretend I wanted to know a lot of things I didn't. But I don't do that now. It was like punching a lame cat to see it hop, and I stopped.

She don't ask me anything, either. Never has since the day Mr. Benson came in our class and asked for a little review, and Martha Cary made trouble, of course.

Miss Sallie was so red and excited by Mr. Benson sitting there beside her that she didn't know what she was doing. She didn't, or she wouldn't have asked me questions, knowing I never say the things I ought. But after a minute she did ask me, fanning just as hard as she could. It was in January.

"Now, Mary Cary, tell us something of the people we have been studying about this winter," she said, "Mention something of Abraham, Isaac, and Jacob, and Peter and Paul. Who was Abraham?"

"Abraham was a coward," I said.

"A what?" And her voice was a little shriek. "A what?"

"A coward. He was! He passed his wife off for his sister, fearing trouble for himself, and not thinking of consequences for her."

"That will do," she said, and she fanned harder than ever, and looked real frightened at Mr. Benson, who was blowing his nose. "Susie Rice, who was Jacob?"

Susie didn't know. Nobody knew, so I spoke again.

"Jacob was a rascal. He deceived his father and stole from his brother. But he prospered and repented, and died prominent."

Mr. Benson got up and said he believed his nose was bleeding, and went out quick, and since then Miss Sallie has never asked me a single question. Not one.

Now I wonder what made Martha speak out like that? Abraham and Jacob were good men who did some bad things, but generally only their goodness is mentioned. While you're living it's apt to be the other way.

But I'm glad the bad is overlooked in time. Maybe that is what God will do with everybody. He'll wipe out all the wrongness and meanness, and see through it to the good. I hope that's the way it's going to be, for that's my only chance.

Since Miss Sallie stopped asking me anything, and I her, I have a lovely time in my mind taking things off the other children and putting them on the Orphans. There's Margaret Evans. In the winter she's always blue and frozen, and I'd give her that Mallory child's velvet coat and gray muff and tippet, and put Margaret's blue cape and calico dress on her.

Poor little Margaret! She's so humble and thankful she gets even less than the rest, it looks like, though I suppose in clothes she has the same allowance, and the difference, maybe, is in herself.

Some people are born to be stepped on, and of steppers there are always a-plenty.

After Sunday-school we walk to the church we're going to, two by two, just alike and all in blue. The minister always mentions us in his prayers, except at St. John's, the prayer-book not providing for Orphans in particular.

When church is over we march home and have dinner, and after dinner we study the lesson for next Sunday and practise hymns until time for the afternoon service. That begins at four, and some of the town ministers preach or talk, generally preach, long and wearisome.

The Episcopal minister gets through in a hurry. We love to have him. He talks so fast we don't half understand, and before we know it he's got his hand up and we hear him saying: "And now to the Father and to the Son--." And the rest is mumbled, but we know he's through and is glad of it, and so are we.

The Presbyterian Sunday is the longest and solemnest, and I always write a new story in my mind when Dr. Moffett preaches. He is very learned, and knows Hebrew and Latin and Greek, but not much about little girls.

Poor Mrs Blamire; she tries to keep awake, but she can't do it; and after the first five minutes she puffs away just as regular as if she were wound up. Once I shut my eyes and tried to puff like her, but I forgot to be careful, and did it so loud the girls came near getting in trouble. Dr. Moffett is deaf, and didn't hear. Miss Bray heard.

But the Baptist minister don't let you sleep on his Sunday. He used to try to make the girls come up and profess, but now he don't ask even that. Just sit where you are and hold up your hand, and when you join the church--any church will answer--you are saved. I don't understand it.

We all like the Methodist minister. I don't think he knows many dead languages. He don't have much time to study, being so busy helping people; but he knows how to talk to us children, and he always makes me wish I wasn't so bad. He always does, and the Mary part of me just rises right up on his Sunday, and Martha is ashamed of herself. He believes in getting better by the love way. So do I.

Miss Katherine is going away next week to stay two months. Going to her army brother's first, and then to the California brother, who's North somewhere. And from the time she told me I've felt like Robinson Crusoe's daughter would have felt, if he'd had one, and gone off and left her on that desert island.

I don't know what we're going to do when she goes away. I could shed gallons of tears, only I don't like tears, and then, too, she might see me. I want her to think I'm glad she's going, for she needs a change. But, oh, the difference her going will make!

I will be nothing but Martha. I know it. Nothing but Martha until she comes back. The Mary part of me is so sick at the thought she hasn't any backbone, and Martha is showing signs already.

And that shows I'm just nothing, for Miss Katherine has taught us, without exactly telling, how we can't do what we ought by wanting. We've got to work. In plain words, its watch and pray, and with me it's the watching that's most important. If I'm not on the lookout, and don't nab Martha right away, praying don't have any effect. I'm a natural pray-er, but on watching I'm poor.

I couldn't make any one understand what Miss Katherine has done for us since she's been here. Some words don't tell things. The nursing when we're sick is only a part, and though she's fixed up one of the rooms just like a hospital-room, with everything so white and clean and sweet in it that it's real joy to be sick, we're not sick often.

It's the keeping us well that's kept her so busy. She's explained so many things to us we didn't know before, she's almost made me like my body. I didn't use to. Not a bit.

It's such a nuisance, and needs so much attention to keep it going right. So often it was freezing cold, or blazing hot, or hungry, and had to be dressed in such ugly clothes that I was ashamed of it. And if ever I could have hung it up in the closet or put it away in a bureau-drawer, I would have done it while I went out and had a good time. But I couldn't do it. I had to take it everywhere I went, and until Miss Katherine came I had mighty little use for it.

But since she's been here the girls are much cleaner, and we don't mind so much not having the things to eat that we like. That is, not quite so much. But almost. When you're downright hungry for the taste of things, it don't satisfy to say to yourself "You don't really need it. Be quiet." And being made of flesh and blood, most of us would rather eat the things we want to than the things we ought to.

But the dining-room is much nicer. We have flowers on the table, and the cooking is better, though we still have prunes.

I loathe prunes.

V
"HERE COMES THE BRIDE!"

I knew when Miss Katherine left I'd be nothing but Martha. That's what I've been--Martha.

She hadn't been gone two days when Mary gave up, and as prompt as possible Martha invented trouble.

It was this way. In the summer we have much more time than in the winter, and the children kept coming to me asking me to make up something, and all of a sudden a play came in my mind. I just love acting. The play was to be the marriage of Dr. Rudd and Miss Bray.

You see, Miss Bray is dead in love with Dr. Rudd--really addled about him. And whenever he comes to see any of the children who are sick she is so solicitous and sweet and smiley that we call her, to ourselves, Ipecac Mollie. Other days, plain Mollie Cottontail. It seemed to me if we could just think him into marrying her, it would be the best work we'd ever done, and I thought it was worth trying.

They say if you just think and think and think about a thing you can make somebody else think about it, too. And not liking Dr. Rudd, we didn't mind thinking her on him, and so we began. Every day we'd meet for an hour and think together, and each one promised to think single, and in between times we got ready.

Becky Drake says love goes hard late in life, and sometimes touches the brain. Maybe that accounts for Miss Bray.

She is fifty-three years old, and all frazzled out and done up with adjuncts. But Dr. Rudd, being a man with not even usual sense, and awful conceited, don't see what we see, and swallows easy. Men are funny--funny as some women.

I don't think he's ever thought of courting Miss Bray. But she's thought of it, and for once we truly tried to help her.

Well, we got ready, beginning two days after Miss Katherine left, and the play came off Friday night, the third of July. In consequence of that play I have been in a retreat, and on the Fourth of July I made a New-Year resolution.

I resolved I would do those things I should not do, and leave undone the things I should. I would not disappoint Miss Bray. She looked for things in me to worry her. She should find them.

Well, I was in that top-story summer-resort for ten days. Put there for reflection. I reflected. And on the difference between Miss Katherine and Miss Bray.

But the play was a corker; it certainly was. We chose Friday night because Miss Jones always takes tea with her aunt that night, and Miss Bray goes to choir practising. I wish everybody could hear her sing! Gabriel ought to engage her to wake the dead, only they'd want to die again.

Dr. Rudd is in the choir, and she just lives on having Friday nights to look forward to.

The ceremony took place in the basement-room where we play in bad weather. It's across from the dining-room, the kitchen being between, and it's a right nice place to march in, being long and narrow.

I was the preacher, and Prudence Arch and Nita Polley, Emma Clark and Margaret Witherspoon were the bridesmaids.

Lizzie Wyatt was the bride, and Katie Freeman, who is the tallest girl in the house, though only fourteen, was the groom.

Katie is so thin she would do as well for one thing in this life as another, so we made her Dr. Rudd.

We didn't have but two men. Miss Webb says they're really not necessary at weddings, except the groom and the minister. Nobody notices them, and, besides, we couldn't get the pants.

I was an Episcopal minister, so I wouldn't need any. Mrs. Blamire's raincoat was the gown, and I cut up an old petticoat into strips, and made bands to go down the front and around my neck. Loulie Prentiss painted some crosses and marks on them with gilt, so as to make me look like a Bishop. I did. A little cent one.

There wasn't any trouble about my costume, because I could soap my hair and make it lie flat, and put on the robe, and there I was. But how to get a pair of pants for Katie Freeman was a puzzle.

Nothing male lives in the Humane. Not even a billy-goat. We couldn't borrow pants, knowing it wouldn't be safe; and what to do I couldn't guess.

Well, the day came, and, still wondering where those pants were to come from, I went out in the yard where a man was painting a window-shutter that had blown off a back window. Right before my eyes was the woodhouse door wide open, and something said to me:

"Walk in."

I walked in; and there in a corner on a woodpile was a real nice pair of pants, and a collar and cravat, and a coat and a tin lunch-bucket, which had been eaten-- the lunch had. And when I saw those pants I knew Katie Freeman was fixed.

They belonged to the man who was painting the shutter.

It was an awful hot day, and he had taken them off in the woodhouse and put on his overalls, and when he wasn't looking I slipped out with them, and went up to Miss Bray's room. She was down-stairs talking to Miss Jones, and I hid them under the mattress of her bed.

I knew when she found they were missing she'd turn to me to know where they were. No matter what went wrong, from the cat having kittens or the chimney smoking, she looked to me as the cause. And if there was to be any searching, No. 4--I sleep in No. 4 when Miss Katherine is away--would be the first thing searched. So I put them under her bed.

I wish Miss Katherine could have seen that man about six o'clock, when the time came for him to go home. She would have laughed, too. She couldn't have helped it.

He is young, and Bermuda Ray says he is in love with Callie Payne, who lives just down the street. He has to pass her house going home, and I guess that's the reason he wore his good clothes and took them off so carefully. But whether that was it or not, he was the rippenest, maddest man I ever saw in my life when he went to put on his pants and there were none to put.

I almost rolled off the porch up-stairs, where I was watching. I never did know before how much a man thinks of his pants.

He soon had Miss Bray and Miss Jones and a lot of the girls out in the yard, and everybody was talking at once; and then I heard him say:

"But I tell you, Miss Bray, I put 'em here, right on this woodpile. And where are they? You run this place, and you are responsible for--"

"Not for pants." And Miss Bray's voice was so shrill it sounded like a broken whistle. "I'm responsible for no man's pants. When a man can't take care of his pants, he shouldn't have them. Besides, you shouldn't have left yours in the wood-house when working in a Female Orphan Asylum." And she glared so at him that the poor male thing withered, and blushed real beautiful.

He's a pretty young man, and I felt sorry for him when Miss Bray snapped so. I certainly did.

"My overalls are my working-pants," he said, real meek-like, and his voice was trembling so I thought he was going to cry. "It's very strange that in a place like this a man's clothes are not safe. I thought--"

"Well, you had no business thinking. Next time keep your pants on." And Miss Bray, who's good on a bluff, pretended like she had been truly injured, and the poor little painter sat down.

Presently his face changed, as if a thought had come into his mind from a long way off, and he said, in another kind of voice:

"I beg your pardon, Miss Bray. I believe I know who done it. It's a friend of mine who tries to be funny every now and then, and calls it joking. I'll choke his liver out of him!" And he settled himself on the woodpile to wait until dark before he went home.

If anybody thinks that wedding was slumpy, they think wrong. It was thrilly. When the bride and groom and the bridesmaids came in, all the girls were standing in rows on either side of the walk, making an aisle in between, and they sang a wedding-song I had invented from my heart.

It was to the Lohengrin tune, which is a little wobbly for words, but they got them in all right, keeping time with their hands. These are the words:

1

Here comes the Bride,
God save the Groom!
And please don't let any chil-i-il-dren come,
For they don't know

How children feel,
Nor do they know how with chil-dren to deal.

2

She's still an old maid,
Though she would not have been
Could she have mar-ri-ed any kind of man.
But she could not.
So to the Humane
She came, and caus-ed a good deal of pain.

3

But now she's here
To be married, and go
Away with her red-headed, red-bearded beau.
Have mercy, Lord,
And help him to bear
What we've been doing this many a year!

And such singing! We'd been practising in the back part of the yard, and humming in bed, so as to get the words into the tune; but we hadn't let out until that night. That night we let go.

There's nothing like singing from your heart, and, though I was the minister and stood on a box which was shaky, I sang, too. I led.

The bride didn't think it was modest to hold up her head, and she was the only silent one. But the bridegroom and bridesmaids sang, and it sounded like the revivals at the Methodist church. It was grand.

And that bride! She was Miss Bray. A graven image of her couldn't have been more like her.

She was stuffed in the right places, and her hair was frizzed just like Miss Bray's. Frizzed in front, and slick and tight in the back; and her face was a purple pink, and powdered all over, with a piece of dough just above her mouth on the left side to correspond with Miss Bray's mole.

And she held herself so like her, shoulders back, and making that little nervous sniffle with her nose, like Miss Bray makes when she's excited, that once I had to wink at her to stop.

The groom didn't look like Dr. Rudd. But she wore men's clothes, and that's the only way you'd know some men were men, and almost anything will do for a groom. Nobody noticed him.

We were getting on just grand, and I was marrying away, telling them what they must do and what they mustn't. Particularly that they mustn't get mad and leave each other, for Yorkburg was very old-fashioned and didn't like changes, and would rather stick to its mistakes than go back on its word. And then I turned to the bride.

"Miss Bray," I said, "have you told this man you are marrying that you are two-faced and underhand, and can't be trusted to tell the truth? Have you told him that nobody loves you, and that for years you have tried to pass for a lamb, when you are an old sheep? And does he know that though you're a good manager on little and are not lazy, that your temper's been ruined by economizing, and that at times, if you were dead, there'd be no place for you? Peter wouldn't pass you, and the devil wouldn't stand you. And does he know he's buying a pig in a bag, and that the best wedding present he could give you would be a set of new teeth? And will you promise to stop pink powder and clean your finger-nails every day? And--"

But I got no further, for something made me look up, and there, standing in the door, was the real Miss Bray.

All I said was--"Let us pray!"

VI
"MY LADY OF THE LOVELY HEART"

Beautiful gloriousness! Miss Katherine has come back!
What a different place some people can make the same place!
Yesterday there wasn't an interesting thing in Yorkburg. Nothing but dust and shabby old houses and poky people who knew nothing to talk about, and to-day--oh, to-day it's dear! I love it!

You see, after that wedding everything went wrong. The girls said it wasn't fair for me to be punished so much more than the rest, and they wanted to tell the Board about it; but for once I agreed with Miss Bray.

"I did it. I made it up and fixed everything, and you all just agreed," I said. "And if anybody has to pay, I'm the one to do it." And I paid all right. Paid to the full. But it's over now, and I'm not going to think about it any more. When a thing is over, that should be the end of it, Miss Katherine says, and with me what she says goes.

Miss Bray is away. If some of her relations liked her well enough to have her stay a few months with them, she could get leave of absence; but she's never been known to stay but four weeks. She's gone to visit her sister somewhere in Fauquier County. Her sister's husband always leaves home for his health when she arrives, and Miss Bray says she thinks it's so queer he has the same kind of spells at the same time every year.

But now Miss Katherine's back, nothing matters. Nothing!

Yesterday I was just a squirrel in a cage. All day long I was saying: "Well, Squirrel, turn your little wheel. That's all you can do; turn your little wheel." And inside I was turning as hard and fast as a sure-enough squirrel turns; but outside I was just mechanical.

I wonder sometimes I don't blaze up right before people's eyes. I'm so often on fire--that is, my mind and heart are--that I think at times my body will surely catch. Thus far it hasn't, but if I don't go somewhere, see something, do something different, it's apt to, and the doctors won't have a name for the new kind of inflammation.

I'm going to die after a while, and I'm so afraid I will do it before I travel some that if I were a boy child I'd go anyhow. But I can't go. That is, not yet.

Miss Katherine has been travelling for two months up North. She's been with her brother and his wife. The wife is sick, or she thinks she is, which Miss Katherine says is a hard disease to cure, and she's kept them moving from place to place.

They wanted Miss Katherine to go to Europe with them this fall, but she isn't going. She's been twice, and says she don't want to go. But I don't believe it's that. I believe it's something else.

But sufficient unto the day is the happiness thereof! I'm going to enjoy her staying, and already everything seems different.

You see, Miss Katherine lives here just for love, and when you do things for love you do them differently from the way you do them for money.

We are just Charity children, some not knowing who they are, I being one of that kind; but she never treats us as if she thinks of that. If we were relations she liked, she couldn't be kinder or nicer, and when a child is in trouble Miss Katherine is the one that's gone to at once.

She is never too tired or too busy to listen, but she's awful firm; and there's no nonsense or sullenness or shamming where she is. She can see through the insides of your soul, up to the top and down to the tip, and in front of her eyes you are just your plain self. Only that, and nothing more. They are gray, her eyes are, with a dark rim around the gray part; and she has the longest black lashes I ever saw. Her hair is black, too, like an Eastern Princess and in the morning when she puts her cap on and her nurse's white dress, which she wears when on duty, I call her to myself, "My Lady of the Lovely Heart," and I could kneel down and say my prayers to her.

I don't, though, for she would tell me pretty quick to get up. She doesn't like things like that, and, of course, it would look queer.

But I don't know anybody who isn't queer about something. Either stupid queer, or silly queer, or smart queer, or beautiful queer, or religious queer, or selfish queer, or some other kind.

Miss Bray is the Queen of Queers.

But Miss Katherine is queer, too. If she wasn't, she wouldn't stay at this Orphan Asylum, just to help us children, and doing it as cheerfully as if she were happier here than she would be anywhere else. If her staying isn't queerness, beautiful queerness, what is it?

I don't understand it, and I don't believe I ever will understand how any one who can get ice-cream will take prunes.

But Miss Katherine has got a way of seeing the funny side of things, and sometimes I can't tell whether she minds prunes and pruny things or not.

I'm sure she does, but she says, when you can't change a thing, don't let it change you, and that an inward disposition is hard on other people.

I don't know what that means, but I think it's the same as saying there's no use in always chewing the rag. Martha is right much inclined to be a chewer.

Miss Webb is, too. She is Miss Katherine's best friend, and I just love to hear her talk.

She always comes once a week, often twice, to spend the evening at the Asylum with Miss Katherine, and sometimes when they think I'm asleep, I'm not. I'd be a nuisance if I kept popping up and saying, "I'm not asleep, speak low." So when I can't, really can't, sleep, though I do try, I hear them talking, and the things Miss Webb says are a great relief to my feelings.

She doesn't come to supper, orphan-asylum suppers being refreshments to stay from, not come to, but nearly always they make something on a chafing-dish. Something that's good, painful good.

Miss Webb says Miss Katherine's stomach has some rights, which is true; and when they begin to cook, I just sleep away, breathing regular and easy, so they won't know I am awake, for fear they might think I am not asleep on purpose.

But I have to hold on to the bed and stuff my ears and nose so as not to hear and smell, for I am that hungry I could eat horse if it had Worcestershire sauce on it. And that is what they put in their things, which shows that in eating, even, Miss Katherine preaches sense and practises taste.

Miss Webb just laughs at theories, and brings all sorts of good things with her. She says doctors have wronged more stomachs than they've ever righted by all this dieting business, and, while there's sense in some of it, there's more nonsense; and as for her, she don't believe in it. I don't know anything about it; but I don't, either.

They always save me some of whatever they make, which I get the next day. But if I could rise out of bed and eat as much as I want out of that chafing-dish, there would be a funeral Miss Bray would like to attend. The corpse would be Mary Cary, died Martha.

There is a screen at the foot of my bed, put there so the light won't bother me and so I won't be seen. And, thinking I am asleep, Miss Katherine and Miss Webb talk on as if I were dead; and it's very interesting the things they talk about.

Of course, Miss Webb came over last night, and, after talking about two hours, she said: "Oh, I forgot to tell you. Lizzie Lane is going to marry Bob Rogers, and right away. I don't suppose you've heard."

"Yes, I have; Lizzie wrote me." And Miss Katherine took the hair-pins out of her hair and let it fall down her back. "What made her change her mind? What is she marrying him for?"

"How do I know?" And Miss Webb tasted the chocolate to see if it was sweet enough.

"How does anybody know what a man is married for? In most cases you can't risk a guess. Lizzie is a woman, therefore 'hath reason or unreason for her act.'"

"How did it happen? What made her change her mind?" and Miss Katherine threw her hair-pins on the bureau and stooped down to get her slippers. "How does Lizzie explain it?"

"She says she was so sleepy she doesn't remember whether she said yes or no. But Bob remembers, and the wedding is to be week after next. He's courted her three times a year for seven years; but since he's been living North he hasn't even written to her, and she didn't know he was in town until he came up that night to see her.

"He stayed until after one o'clock, and didn't mention marriage. But as he got up to go he told her his house was going to send him on a six months' trip to Japan. If she would marry him and go, say so. If not, say that, too, but for the last time. Lizzie said she'd go."

Miss Katherine fastened her kimono, put her feet up on the chair in front of her, and clasped her hands behind her head.

"I don't wonder at the unhappy marriages," she said. "The queer part is there aren't more of them. Why did Bob wait eight years to talk to Lizzie like this? Why is it a man has so little understanding of a woman?"

"Why? Because he's a Man. The Lord made him, and there must be some reason for him; but even the Lord must sometimes get worn out at his dumbness. However--"

She stopped, for the chocolate was boiling over; then she began to sing:

"Before marriage, men love most.
After marriage, women best.
Marriage many changes makes--
Heart is happy or heart breaks."

And she sang it so many times that I went to sleep and dreamed the dream I love most.

I see hundreds and hundreds of little creatures (they are the Mary part of little children), and they are afraid and shivering and standing about, not knowing where to go or what to do. And then Miss Katherine is in the midst of them, smiling and beckoning, and they follow and follow, and wings come out. Just tiny ones at first, and then larger and larger, and presently they fly all around her, and she points the way, smiling and cheering.

And then they rise higher and higher, and off they go, and she is alone. Tired out but glad, because she taught them how to use their wings.

VII
"STERILIZED AND FERTILIZED"

This is Sunday, and we have done all the usual Sunday things. There won't be another for seven days. For that we give thanks in our hearts, but not out loud.

This was Presbyterian Sunday. Miss Bray is a Presbyterian.

It is a solemn thing to be a Presbyterian, and easy for the mind, too. Everything is fixed, and there is no unfixing. You are saved or you are not saved, and you will never know which it is until after you are dead and find out. Miss Bray believes she is saved, and she takes liberties. She also thinks everything is as God ordered it, and she believes God ordered poor Mrs. Craddock to die--that is, took her away. I don't. I think it was that last baby.

She had had twelve, and the thirteenth just wore her out at the thought. There being nobody to do anything for her, she got up and cooked breakfast in her stocking feet when the baby was only a week old, and that night she had the influenza, and the next pneumonia. On the sixth day she was dead, and so was the baby. They forgot to feed it.

I don't believe God ever took any mothers away intentional. He never would have made them so necessary if He had meant to take them away when they were most needed. When they go I believe He is sorry.

I don't know how to explain it. Nobody does, though a lot try. But I know He sees it bigger than we do, and maybe He is working at something that isn't finished yet.

Minnie Peters is real sick. Miss Katherine has put her in the hospital-room, and is staying in there with her.

I am all alone by myself to-night. I don't like aloneness at night. It makes you pay too much attention to your feelings, which Miss Katherine says is the cause of more trouble in this world than all other diseases put together.

She says, too, that what we feel about a thing is very often different from the way other people feel about it. And when you don't agree with people, the only thing you can be sure about is that they don't agree with you. I believe that's true. Not being by nature much of an agree-er, and having feelings I hope others don't, I would be a walking argument if Miss Katherine hadn't stopped me and explained some things I didn't realize before.

Last night, being by myself, and not being able to go to sleep, I wrote a piece of poetry.

Miss Katherine says it's hard to forgive people who think they write poetry, so I won't show her this. But it does relieve you to write down a lot of woozy nothing that is somehow like you feel. This is the poem--I mean the verses:

1

Out upon life's ocean vast,
With the current drifting fast,
I am sailing. Oh, alas,
'Tis a lonely feeling!

2

Why was such a trip e'er started
On a pathway all uncharted?
Why from loved ones was I parted?
Who will answer? Who?

3

None will answer. So I'll see
What there is on this journey (journee)
That will bring good-luck to me--

I'll look out and see!

I hope Minnie isn't going to be sick long. She is the first girl to be really ill since Miss Katherine came. It makes you feel so queer in the throat to know somebody is truly sick.

A lot of the girls have been sick a little with colds and small and unserious diseases in the past year. But Miss Katherine says it's her business to keep us well, not just get us well after we're sick, and she's certainly done it. We've been weller than we ever were in our lives, and no medicine taken. Just plain common-sense regulations.

I wonder what's the matter with Minnie? The doctor hasn't said, but Miss Katherine is uneasy, and she won't let anybody come in the room. She hasn't been out herself since yesterday.

*   *   *   *   *

My, but we've had a time lately!

We've been fumigated and sterilized and fertilized so much that we are better prepared for the happy-land than we ever were before. But the danger of anybody going to it right away is over.

Minnie Peters has had scarlet fever, and the commotion made her real famous.

Miss Katherine knew it from the first, but Dr. Rudd wouldn't believe it until he had to, and Yorkburg got so excited it hasn't talked of anything else for weeks.

Minnie was awful ill. Two days and two nights they didn't think she would live, and for three weeks Miss Katherine didn't leave the room. If it hadn't been for her Minnie would be dead.

Miss Katherine's room has been closed since they first found out it was really scarlet fever Minnie had, and I have been in No. 4 again. She is going away to spend a week with Miss Webb. Going to-morrow.

I am so glad she is going. All of us are glad, for she has had to do something which shows whether you are a Christ-kind Christian or the usual kind, and she is tired out. She won't admit it, though, and laughs and kisses her hand over the banister, which is all the closer we have seen her yet.

Miss Bray was scared to death. She didn't offer to share the nursing, but she made excuses a-plenty for not doing it. Miss Bray is a church Christian. You couldn't make her miss going to church. She thinks she'd have bad luck if she did.

VIII
MARY CARY'S BUSINESS

This is a busy time of the year, and things are moving. I'm in business. The Apple and Entertainment business.

The reason I went in business was to make money, and the money was to buy Christmas presents with.

I didn't have a cent. Not one. Christmas was coming. Money wasn't. And what's the use of Christmas if you can't give something to somebody?

Religion is the only thing I know of that you can get without money and without price, and even that you can't keep without both. Not being suitable to the season, I couldn't give that away, even if I had it to spare, and wondering what to do almost made me sick.

I thought and thought until my brain curdled. I looked over everything I had to see if there was a thing I could sell. There wasn't. I couldn't tell Miss Katherine, knowing she'd fix up some way to give me some and pretend I was earning it; and then, one day, when she was out, I locked myself in her room, and Martha gave Mary such a spanking talk that Mary moved.

Everything Martha had suggested before, Mary had some excuse for not doing. Mary is lazy at times, and, as for pride, she's full of it. Martha generally gives the trouble, but Mary needs plain truth every now and then, and that day she got it. When the talk was over, there was a plan settled on, and the plan was this.

Each day in December we have an apple for dinner. Mr. Riley sends us several barrels every winter, and, as they won't keep, we have one apiece until they're gone.

We don't have to eat them at the table, and when Martha told Mary you could do anything you wanted if you wanted to hard enough--except raise the dead, of course--the idea came that I could sell my apple. And right away came the thought of the boy I could sell it to. John Maxwell is his name.

He goes to our Sunday-school and is fifteen, and croaks like a bull-frog. Ugly? Pug-dog ugly; but he's awful nice, and for a boy has real much sense.

His father owns the shoe-factory, and has plenty of money. I know, for he told me he had five cents every day to get something for lunch, and fifty cents a week to do anything he wants with. His mother gives it to him.

Well, the next Sunday he came over to talk, like he always does after Sunday-school is out, and I said, real quick, Mary giving signs of silliness:

"I'm in business. Did you know it?"

"No," he said. "What kind? Want a partner?"

"I don't. I want customers. I'm in the Apple business. I have an apple every day. It's for sale. Want to buy it?"

"What's the price?" Then he laughed. "I'm from New Jersey. What's it worth?"

"It's worth a cent. As you're from New Jersey, I charge you two. Take it?"

"I do." And he started to hand the money out.

But I told him I didn't want pay in advance. And then we talked over how the apple could be put where he could get it, and the money where I could. We decided on a certain hole in the Asylum fence John knew about, and every evening that week I put my apple there and found his two pennies. On Saturday night I had fourteen cents. Wasn't that grand? Fourteen cents!

But the next Sunday there came near being trouble. Roper Gordon--he's John Maxwell's cousin--had heard about the apple selling. He told me I wasn't charging enough, and that he'd pay three cents for it.

"I'll be dogged if you will," said John. "I'm cornering that apple, and I'll meet you. I'll give four."

"All right," I said. "I'm in business to make money. I'm not charging for worth, but for want. The one who wants it most will pay most. It can go at four."

"No, it can't!" said Roper. His father is rich, too. He's the Vice-President of the Factory, and Roper puts on lots of airs. He thinks money can do anything.

"I'll give five. Apples in small lots come high, and selected ones higher. John is a close buyer, and isn't toting square."

"That's a lie!" said John, and he lit out with his right arm and gave Roper such a blow that my heart popped right out on my tongue and sat there. Scared? I was weak as a dead cat.

But I grabbed John and pulled him behind me before Roper could hit back, and then in some way they got outside, and I heard afterward John beat Roper to a jelly.

I don't blame him. If any one were to say I wasn't square, I'd fight, too.

When you don't fight, it's because what is said is true, and you're afraid it will be found out. And a coward. Good Lord!

Anyhow, after that I got five cents a day for my apple. John put six cents in, raising Roper, he said, but I wouldn't keep but five.

"I can't," I said. "I hate my conscience, for even in business it pokes itself in. But five cents is all I can take."

"Which shows you're new in business, or you'd take the other fellow's skin if he had to have what you've got. And I'm bound to have that apple. Bound to!" And he dug the toe of his shoe so deep in the dirt he could have put his foot in. We were down at the fence, where I went to tell him he mustn't leave but five cents any more.

The Apple business was much easier than the Entertainment business; but I enjoyed both. Making money is exciting. I guess that's why men love to make it.

I made in all $2.34. One dollar and fifty cents on entertaining, and eighty-four cents on apples.

The entertaining was this way. Mrs. Dick Moon is twin to the lady who lived in a shoe. Her house isn't far from the Asylum, and I like her real much; but she isn't good on management. Everything on the place just runs over everything else, and nothing is ever ready on time.

She has money--that is, her husband has, which Miss Katherine says isn't always the same thing. And she has servants and a graphophone and a pianola, but she doesn't really seem to have anything but children, and they are everywhere.

They are the sprawly kind that lie on their stomachs and kick their heels, and get under your feet and on your back. And their mouths always have molasses or sugar in the corners, and their noses have colds, and their hands are that sticky they leave a print on everything they touch.

But they aren't mean-bad, just bad because they don't know what to do, and they beg me to stay and play with them when Miss Jones sends me over with a message. Sometimes I do, and the day Martha gave Mary such a rasping about making money, another thought came besides the apples, and I went that afternoon to see Mrs. Moon.

"Mrs. Moon," I said, "the children have colds and can't go out. If Miss Bray will let me, would you like me to come over and entertain them during our play-hour? It's from half-past four to half-past five. I'll come every day from now until Christmas, and I charge twenty-five cents a week for it."

I knew my face was rambler red. I hated to mention money, but I hated worse not to have any to buy Miss Katherine a present with. If she thought twenty-five cents a week too high she could say so. But she didn't.

"Mercy, Mary Cary!" she said, "do you mean it? Would I like you to come? Would I? I wish I could buy you!" And she threw her arms around me and kissed me so funny I thought she was going to cry.

"Of course I want you," she went on, after wiping her nose. She had a cold, too. "You can manage the children better than I, and if you knew what one quiet hour a day meant to the mother of seven, all under twelve, you'd charge more than you're doing. I'll see Miss Bray to-morrow."

She saw, and Miss Bray let me come.

Mrs. Moon is a member of the Board, and Mr. Moon is rich. Miss Bray never sleeps in waking time.

Well, when Mrs. Moon paid me for the first week, she gave me fifty cents instead of twenty-five, and I wouldn't take it.

"But you've earned it," she said, putting it back in my hand, and giving it a little pat--a little love pat. "You didn't say you were coming on Sundays, and you came. Sunday is the worst day of all. I nearly go crazy on Sunday. No, child, don't think you're getting too much. One doctor's visit would be two dollars, and the prescription forty cents, anyhow. The children would be on the bed, and my head splitting, and Mammy as much good in keeping them quiet as a cackling hen. I feel like I'm cheating in only paying fifty cents. Each nap was worth that. I wish I could engage you by the year!" And she gave me such a squeeze I almost lost my breath.

But they are funny, those Moon children. Sarah Sue is the oldest, and nobody ever knows what Sarah Sue is going to say.

Yesterday I made them tell me what they were going to buy for their mother's and father's Christmas presents, and the things they said were queer. As queer as the presents some grown people give each other.

"I'm going to give father a set of tools," said Bobbie. "I saw 'em in Mr. Blakey's window, and they'll cut all right. They cost eighty-five cents."

"What are you going to give your father tools for?" I asked. "He's not a boy."

"But I am." And Bobbie jumped over a chair on Billy's back. "You said yourself you ought always to give a person a thing you'd like to have, and I'd like those tools. They're the bulliest set in Yorkburg. I'm going to give mother a little yellow duck. That's at Mr. Blakey's, too."

"It don't cost but five cents," said Sarah Sue, and she looked at Bobbie as if he were not even the dust of the earth. Then she handed me her list.

"But, Sarah Sue," I said, after I'd read it, "you've got seventy-five cents down here for your mother and only fifty for your father. Do you think it's right to make a difference?"

"Yes, I do." And Sarah Sue's big brown eyes were as serious as if 'twere funeral flowers she was selecting. "You see, it's this way. I love them both seventy-five cents' worth, but I don't think I ought to give them the same. Father is just my father by marriage, but Mother's my mother by bornation. I think mothers ought always to have the most."

I think so, too.

IX
LOVE IS BEST

Christmas is over. I feel like the parlor grate when the fire has gone out. But it was a grand Christmas, the grandest we've ever known. It came on Christmas Day. From the time we got up until we went to bed we were so happy we forgot we were Charity children; and no matter whatever happens, we've got one beautiful time to look back on.

Miss Katherine says a beautiful memory is a possession no one can take from you, and it's one of the best possessions you can have. I think so, too. She's made all my memories. All. I mean the precious ones.

Everybody in this Orphan Asylum had a present from somebody outside. Even me, who might as well be that man in the Bible, Melchesey something, who didn't have beginning or end, or any relations.

I had fourteen from outside. Some I hid, because I didn't want the girls to know, several not getting more than one, and hardly any more than three or four.

Those who had the heart to give them didn't have the money, and those who had the money didn't have the heart. Being so busy with their own they forgot to remember, and if it hadn't been for Miss Katherine and her friends this last Christmas would have been like all others.

Her Army brother's wife sent a box full of all sorts of pretty Indian things, she being in the wild West near the Indians who made them. And she sent ten dolls, all dressed, for the ten youngest girls.

She is awful busy, having three children and not much money; but Miss Katherine says busy people make time, and those who have most to do, do more still.

She sent me the darlingest little bedroom slippers with fur all around the top. And in them she put a little note that made me cry and cry and cry, it was so dear and mothery. I don't know what made me cry, but I couldn't help it. I couldn't.

She doesn't know me except from what Miss Katherine writes, and I wonder why she wrote that note. But everybody is good to me--that is, nearly everybody.

It certainly makes a difference in your backbone when people are kind and when they are not. I don't believe unkindness and misfortune and suffering will ever make me good. If anybody is mean to me, I'm stifferer than a lamp-post, and you couldn't make me cry. But when any one is good to me, I haven't a bit of firmness, and am no better than a caterpillar.

I got thirty-one presents this year. Thirty-one! I didn't know I had so many friends in Yorkburg, and my heart was so bursting with surprise and gratitude it just ached. Ached happy.

We are not often allowed to make regular visits, but I have lots of little talks informal on errands, or messages, or passing; and as I know almost everybody by sight, I have a right large speaking acquaintance. With some people, Miss Katherine says, that's the safest kind to have.

You see, Yorkburg is a very small place. Just three long streets and some short ones going across. Scratching up everything, it hasn't got three thousand people in it. A lot of them are colored.

But it's very old and historic. Awful old; so is everything in it. As for its blue blood, Mrs. Hunt says there's more in Yorkburg than any place of its size in America.

Most of the strangers who come here, though, seem to prefer to pass on rather than stop, and Miss Webb thinks it's on account of the blood. A little red mixed in might wake Yorkburg up, she says, and that's what it needs--to know the war is over and the change has come to stay.

But I love Yorkburg, and most of the people are dear. Some queer. Old Mrs. Peet is. Her husband has been dead forty years, but she still keeps his hat on the rack for protection, and whenever any one goes to see her after dark she always calls him, as if he were upstairs.

She lives by herself and is over seventy, and she's pretended so long that he's living that they say she really believes he is. She almost makes you believe it, too.

Miss Bray sent me there one night. She wanted some cherry-bounce for Eliza Green, who had an awful pain, and after I'd knocked, I'd have run if I'd dared.

In the hall I could hear Mrs. Peet pounding on the floor with her stick. Then her little piping voice:

"Mr. Peet, Mr. Peet, you'd better come down! There's some one at the door! You'd better come down, Mr. Peet!"

"It's just Mary Cary!" I called. "Miss Bray sent me, Mrs. Peet. She wants some cherry-bounce."

"Oh, all right, Mr. Peet. You needn't bother to come down. It's just little Mary Cary." And she opened the door a tiny crack and peeped through.

"Mr. Peet isn't very well to-night," she said. "He's taken fresh cold. But you can come in."

I came; but I didn't want to. And if Mr. Peet had come down those steps and shaken hands I wouldn't have been surprised. It's certainly strange how something you know isn't true seems true; and Mr. Peet, dead forty years, seemed awful alive that night. Every minute I thought he'd walk in.

She likes you to think he's living at night. Every day she goes to his grave, which is in the churchyard right next to where she lives; but at night he comes back to life to her. She's so lonely, I think it's beautiful that he comes.

I make out like I think he comes, too, and I always send him my love, and ask how his rheumatism is. I tell you, Martha don't dare smile when I do it. She don't even want to.

And, don't you know, old Mrs. Peet sent me a Christmas present, too. A pair of mittens. She knit them herself. It was awful nice of her.

I don't know how big the check was that Miss Katherine's billionaire brother sent her to spend on the children's Christmas, but it must have been a corker. The things she bought with it cost money, and the change it made in the Asylum was Cinderellary. It was.

She bought a carpet for the parlor, and some curtains for the windows, and a bookcase of books.

For the dining-room she bought six new tables and sixty chairs. They were plain, but to sit at a table with only ten at it instead of forty, as I'd been sitting for many years, was to have a proud sensation in your stomach. Mine got so gay I couldn't eat at the first meal.

To have a chair all to yourself, after sitting on benches so old they were worn on both edges, was to feel like the Queen of Sheba, and I felt like her. I could have danced up and down the table, but instead I said grace over and over inside. I had something to say it for. All of us did.

Besides a present, each of us had a new dress. It was made of worsted--real worsted, not calico; and that morning after breakfast, and after everything had been cleaned up, we put on our new dresses and came down in the parlor.

And such a fire as there was in it!

It sputtered and flamed, and danced and blazed, and crackled and roared. Oh, it knew it was Christmas, that fire did, and the mistletoe and holly and running cedar knew it, too!

At first, though, the children felt so stiff and funny in their new-shaped dresses made like other children's that they weren't natural, so I pretended we were having a soiree, and I went round and shook hands with every one.

They got to laughing so at the names I gave them--names that fit some, and didn't touch others by a thousand years--that the stiffness went. And if in all Yorkburg there was a cheerfuller room or a happier lot of children that Christmas Day than we were, we didn't hear of it. I don't believe there was, either.

The reason we enjoyed this Christmas so was because it was on Christmas Day.

Our celebrations had always been after Christmas, and Christmas after Christmas is like cold buckwheat cakes and no syrup. Like an orange with the juice all gone.

As for the tree, it was a spanker. We were dazed dumb for a minute when the parlor doors leading into the sewing-room were opened. But never being able to stay dumb long, I commenced to clap. Then everybody clapped. Clapped so hard half the candles went out.

There wasn't a soul on the place that didn't get a present. This tree was Miss Katherine's, not the Board's, and the presents bought with the brother's money were things we could keep. Not things to put away and pass on to somebody else next year. I almost had a fit when I found I had roller-skates and a set of books too. Think of it! Roller-skates and books! The rich brother sent those himself, and I'm still wondering why.

This was Miss Katherine's second Christmas with us, but the first she had managed herself. Last Christmas she had been at the Asylum such a short time she kept quiet, and just saw how things were done. And not done. But this year she asked if she could provide the entertainment, and the difference in these last two Christ-mases was like the difference in the way things are done from love and duty.

And oh! love is so much the best!

I do believe I was the happiest child in all the world that day, and I didn't come out of that cloud of glory until night. Mrs. Christopher Pryor took me out.

She had come over with some of the Board ladies to see the tree and things, and as she was going home I heard her say:

"I don't approve of all this. Not at all. Not at all. These children have had a more elaborate Christmas than mine. They've had as good a dinner, a handsomer tree, and as many presents as some well-off people. It's all nonsense, putting notions in their heads when they're as poor as poverty itself and have their living to make. I don't approve of it. Not at all."

She bristled so stiff and shook her head so vigorous that the little jet ornaments on her bonnet just tinkled like bells, and one fell off.

Mrs. Christopher Pryor is one of the people who would like to tell the Lord how to run this earth. She could run it. That He lets the rain fall and sun shine on everybody alike is a thing she don't approve of either. As for poor people, she thinks they ought to be thankful for breath, and not expect more than enough to keep it from going out for good.

She's very decided in her views, and never keeps them to herself. It's the one thing she gives away. Everything else she holds on to with such a grip that it keeps her upper lip so pressed down on her under lip that she breathes through her nose most of the time.

She's a very curious shape. Being stout, she has to hold her head up to keep her chin off her fatness; and she goes in so at the waist, coming out top and bottom, that you would think something in her would get jammed out of place. You really would.

There are seven daughters. No sons. The boys call their place Hen-House. There is a husband, but nobody seems to notice him; and when with his wife, he always walks behind.

Miss Webb says she's sorry for a man whose wife is too active in the church. Mrs. Pryor is. She leads all the responses; and as for the chants, she takes them right out of the choir's mouth and soars off with them.

I never could bear her; and when I heard her say those words to Mrs. Marsden, I came right down to earth and was Martha Cary in a minute. I'd been Mary all day, and, like a splash in a mud-puddle, she made me Martha; and I heard myself say:

"No, Mrs. Pryor, we know you don't approve. You never yet have let a child here forget she was a Charity child, and only people who make others happy will approve."

Then I walked away as quiet as a Nun's daughter. But I was burning hot all the same, and so surprised at the way Martha spoke, so serious and unlike the way she usually speaks when mad, that I had to go on the back porch and make snowballs and throw hard at something before I was all right again.

But I wouldn't let it ruin my beautiful day. I wouldn't.

That night, when I went to bed, I was so tired out with happiness I couldn't half say my prayers. But I knew God understood. He let the Christ-child be born poor and lowly, so He could understand about Charity children, and everybody else who goes wrong because they don't know how to go right. So I just thanked Him, and thanked Him in my heart.

And when Miss Katherine kissed me good-night and tucked me in bed, she said I'd made her have a beautiful Christmas. That I'd helped everybody and kept things from dragging, because I had enjoyed it so myself, and been so enthusiastic, and she was so glad I was born that way.

I thought she was making fun, it was so ridiculous, thanking me, little Mary Cary, who hadn't done a thing but be glad and seen that nobody was forgot.

But she wasn't making fun, and I went off to sleep and dreamed I was in a place called the Love-Land, where everybody did everything just for love. Which shows it was a dreamland, for on earth there're Brays and Pryors, and people too busy to be kind. And in that Love-Land everything was done the other way, just backward from our way, and yourself came second instead of first.

X
THE REAGAN BALL

I t is snowing fast and furious to-day. It's grand to watch it. I love miracles, and it's a miracle to see an ugly place turn into a palace of marble and silver with diamond decorations. That's what the Asylum is to-day. I certainly would like to have seen the Reagan ball. Miss Webb says it was the best show ever given in Yorkburg, and she enjoyed it, being particular fond of freaks.

Miss Katherine didn't want to go, but Miss Webb made her. For weeks that Reagan ball had been talked about, and Yorkburg knew things about it that had never been known about parties before, money not often being mentioned here.

Everybody knew what this ball was going to cost. Knew the supper was coming from New York, with white waiters and kid gloves. And what Mrs. Reagan and her daughters were going to wear. That their dresses had been made in Europe, and that Mrs. Hamner hadn't been invited, and that more money was coming to Yorkburg in the shape of one man than had ever been in it altogether before.

If I just could have put myself invisible on a picture-frame and looked down on that fleeting show I would have done it. But not being able to work that miracle, I just heard what was going round, and it was very interesting, the things I heard.

Miss Webb and Miss Katherine and I think just alike about Mrs. Reagan. I know, for I heard them talking one night just before the ball.

"But why in the name of Heaven should I go if I don't want to?" said Miss Katherine, and she put her feet on the fender and lay back in her big rose-covered chair. "I don't like her, or her family, the English she speaks, or the books she reads. Why, then, should I go to her parties? I'm not going!"

"Oh yes, you are." And Miss Webb put some more coal on the fire and made it blaze. "Knowledge of life requires a knowledge of humanity In all its subdivisions.

Mrs. Reagan is a new sub. As a curio, she's worth the price. You couldn't keep me from her show."

"But she's such a snob. When a woman does not know her grandfather's first name on her mother's side and talks of people not being in her set, Christian charity does not require you to visit her. I agree with Mrs. Rodman. People like that ought to be let alone."

"But Mrs. Rodman isn't going to let them alone. Not for a minute. The only thing that goes on among them that she doesn't know is what she can't find out. She met me this morning, and asked me if I'd heard how many people had gotten here, and when I said no, she made me come in Miss Patty's store, and told me all she'd been able to discover.

"'There are eighteen guests already,' she said, 'and nearly all have rooms to themselves. They tell me it's the fashion now for husbands and wives not to see each other until breakfast, and not then if the wife wants hers in bed.' And the way she lifted her chin and eyebrows would be dangerous for you to try.

"'I tell you it's a reflection on Yorkburg's mode of life,' she went on. 'For two hundred years people have come and gone in this town, and rooms have never been mentioned. But this is a degenerate age. Degenerate! Scandalous wealth shouldn't be recognized, and I don't intend to countenance it myself!'

"But she will." And Miss Webb took up her muff to go. "She bought a pair of cream-colored kid gloves from Miss Patty, and she's going to wear them at that ball. You couldn't keep her away."

And she was there. The first one, they say. She had on the dress her Grandmother wore when her great-grandfather was minister to something in Europe; and when she sailed around the rooms with the big, high comb in her hair that was her great-great-grandmother's, Miss Webb says she was the best side-show on the grounds.

But if you were to take a gimlet and bore a hole in Mrs. Rodman's head, you couldn't make her believe anybody would smile at Her.

She was Mrs. General Rodman, born Mason, and the best blood in Virginia was in her veins. Also in her father's, as she put on his tombstone.

Outside of Virginia she didn't think anybody was really anything. Of course, she knew there were other states where things were done that made money, but she'd just wave her hand if you mentioned them.

As for a Yankee! I wouldn't like to put in words what she does think of a Yankee.

She lost a husband and two brothers and a father and four nephews and an uncle in the war; and all her money; and her house had to be sold; and her baby died before its father saw it; and, of course, that makes a difference. It makes a Yankee real personal.

But Miss Katherine don't feel that way about Yankees. Each of her brothers married one, and she don't seem to mind.

Miss Katherine went to the ball, too. She gave in, after all, and went.

I wish you could have seen her when she was dressed and all ready to go. She had on a long, white satin dress, low neck and short sleeves, with little trimming and no jewelry. And she looked so tall and beautiful, and so something I didn't have a name for, that I was afraid, and my heart beat so thick and fast I thought she'd hear.

I hated it. Hated that satin dress, and the places where she wore it when away from the Asylum; and I sat up in bed, for lying down it was hard to breathe.

Presently she turned from the fire where she had been standing, looking in, and came toward me and kissed me good-night.

In her face was something I had never seen before--something so quiet and proud that I couldn't sleep for a long time after she went away.

It wasn't just the same as the remembrance look I had seen several times before, when she forgot she wasn't by herself. It was prouder than that, and it meant something that didn't get better--just worse.

What was it? If it's a man, who is he? He must be living, for it isn't the look that means something is dead. It means something that won't die, but is never, never going to be told.

XI
FINDING OUT

This world is a hard place to live in. I wish somebody would tell me what we are born for anyway, and what's the use of living.

There are so many things that hurt, and you get so mixed up trying to understand, that if you don't keep busy you'll spend your life guessing at a puzzle that hasn't any answer.

Miss Katherine has gone away. Gone to stay two months, anyhow. Maybe three.

Her Army brother, the one who is a Captain, has been sent to Texas, and his wife and children were taken ill as soon as they got there.

Of course, they sent for Miss Katherine; that is, asked her by telegraph if she wouldn't come. She went. And she'll be going to somebody all her life, for she's the kind that is turned to when things go wrong.

Miss Webb is awful worried. She says a cool head and a warm heart are always worked to death, and the person who has them is forever on call.

Miss Katherine has them.

She had to go, of course. We were not sick, except a few snifflers. We didn't exactly need her, and her brother did; but oh the difference her being away makes!

Three months of doing without her is like three months of daylight and no sunlight. It's like things to eat that haven't any taste; like a room in which the one you wait for never comes.

I am back in No. 4, in one of the thirteen beds. My body goes on doing the same things. Gets up at five o'clock. Dresses, cleans, prays, eats, goes to school, eats, sews, plays, eats, studies, goes to bed. And that's got to be done every day in the same way it was done the day before.

But it's just my body that does them. Outside I am a little machine wound up; inside I am a thousand miles away, and doing a thousand other things. Some day I am going to blow up and break my inside workings, for I wasn't meant to run regular and on time. I wasn't.

What was I meant for? I don't know. But not to be tied to a rope. And that's what I am. Tied to a rope. If I were a boy I'd cut it.

*　　*　　*　　*　　*

I am almost crazy! A wonderful thing has happened. I am so excited my breathing is as bad as old Miss Betsy Hays's. I believe I know who I am.

My heart is jumping and thumping and carrying on so that it makes my teeth chatter; and as I can't tell anybody what I've heard, I am likely to die from keeping it to myself.

I am *not* going to die until I find out. If I did I would be as bad off in heaven as on earth. Even an angel would prefer to know something about itself.

I'm like Miss Bray now. I'm counting on going to heaven. Otherwise it wouldn't make any difference who I was, as one more misery don't matter when you're swamped in miserableness. I suppose that's what hell is: Miserableness.

What are you when you don't go to heaven?

But that's got nothing to do with how I found out who I am. It's like Martha, though: always butting in with questions no Mary on earth could answer.

Well, the way I found out was one of those mysterious ways in which God works his wonders. Yesterday afternoon I asked Miss Bray if I could go over and play with the Moon children, three of whom are sick, and she said I might. We were in the nursery, which is next to Mrs. Moon's bedroom, and she and the lady from Michigan, who is visiting her, were talking and paying no attention to us. Presently something the lady said--her name is Mrs. Grey--made everything in me stop working, and my heart gave a little click like a clock when the pendulum don't swing right.

She was sitting with her back to the door, which was open, and I could see her, but she couldn't see me. All of a sudden she put down her sewing and looked at Mrs. Moon as if something had just come to her.

"Elizabeth Moon, I believe I know that child's uncle," she said. "Ever since you told me about her something has been bothering me. Didn't you say her mother had a brother who years ago went West?"

"Hush," said Mrs. Moon, and she nodded toward me. "She'll hear you, and the ladies wouldn't like it."

She lowered her voice so I couldn't hear all she said, but I heard something about its being the only thing Yorkburg ever did keep quiet about. And only then because everybody felt so sorry for her. In a flash I knew they were talking about me.

After the first understanding, which made everything in me stop, everything got moving, and all my inward workings worked double quick. Why my heart didn't get right out on the floor and look up at me. I don't know. I kept on talking and making up wild things just to keep the children quiet, but I had to hold myself down to the floor. To help, I put Billy and Kitty Lee both in my lap.

What I wanted to do was to go to Mrs. Moon and say: "I am twelve and a half, and I've got the right to know. I want to hear about my uncle. I don't want to know him, he not caring to know me." But before I could really think Mrs. Grey spoke again.

"He has no idea his sister left a child. He told me she married very young, and died a year afterward; and he had heard nothing from her husband since. As soon as I go home I am going to tell him. I certainly am."

"You had better not," said Mrs. Moon. "It's been thirteen years since he left Yorkburg, and, as he has never been back, he evidently doesn't care to know any-thing about it. I don't think the ladies would like you to tell. They are very proud of having kept so quiet out of respect to her father's wishes. If Parke Alden had wanted to learn anything, he could have done it years ago."

"But I tell you he doesn't know there's anything to learn." And the Michigan lady's voice was as snappy as the place she came from. "I know Dr. Alden well," she went on. "He's operated on me twice, and I've spent weeks in his hospital. When he tells me it's best for my head to come off--off my head is to come. And when a man can make people feel that way about him, he isn't the kind that's not square on four sides.

"I tell you, he doesn't know about this child. He's often talked to me about

Yorkburg, knowing you were my cousin. He told me of his sister running away with an actor and marrying him, and dying a year later. Also of his father's death and the sale of the old home, and of many other things. There's no place on earth he loves as he does Virginia. He doesn't come back because there's no one to come to see specially. No real close kin, I mean. The changes in the place where you were born make a man lonelier than a strange city does, and something seems to keep him away."

"You say he doesn't know his sister left a child?" Mrs. Moon put down the needle she was trying to thread, and stuck it in her work. "Why doesn't he know?"

"Why should he? Who was there to tell him, if a bunch of women made up their minds he shouldn't know? He wrote to his sister again and again, but whether his letters ever reached her he never knew. He thinks not, as it was unlike her not to write if they were received.

"Travelling from place to place with her actor husband, who, he said, was a 'younger son Englishman,' the letters probably miscarried, and not for months after her death did he know she was dead."

"We didn't, either," interrupted Mrs. Moon. "In fact, we heard it through Parke, who went West after his father's death. He wrote Roy Wright, telling him about it."

"Who is Roy Wright, and where is he, that he didn't tell Dr. Alden about the child?"

"Oh, Roy's dead. I believe Mary Alden's marriage broke Roy's heart; that is, if a man's heart can be broken. He had been in love with her all her life. Not just loved her, but in love with her. His house was next to the Aldens', where the Reagans now live, and Major Alden and General Wright were old friends, each anxious for the match. When Mary ran away at seventeen and married a man her father didn't know, I tell you Yorkburg was scared to death."

"Do you remember it?"

"Remember! I should think I did. I cried for two weeks. Nearly ruined my eyes. Mary and I were deskmates at Miss Porterfield's school, and I adored her. I really did. So did Dick Moon." She stopped. Then: "Like most women, I'm a compromise," and she laughed. But it was a happy laugh. Mrs. Grey smiled too.

"Was Mary Alden engaged to Roy Wright when she married the other man?" she asked. "Tell me all about her."

"No, she wasn't. Mary Alden was incapable of deceit, and Roy Wright knew she didn't love him. He knew she was never going to marry him. Poor Roy! He was as gentle and sweet and patient as Mary was high-spirited and beautiful, and the last type on earth to win a woman of Mary's temperament. She wanted to be mastered, and Roy could only worship."

"And her father--what did he do?"

"Do? The Aldens are not people who 'do' things. The day after the news came, he and General Wright walked arm and arm all over Yorkburg, and their heads were high; but oh, my dear, it was pitiful. They didn't know, but they were clinging to each other, and the Major's face was like death."

"Didn't some one say he had been pretty strict with her? Held too tight a rein?"

"Yes, he had, and he deserved part of his suffering. His pride was inherited, and Mary could go with no one whose great-grandparents he didn't know about. But Mary cared no more for ancestors than she did for Hottentots. When she met this Mr. Cary, a young English actor, at a friend's house in Baltimore, she made no inquiry as to whether he had any, and fell in love at once. He was a gentleman, however. That was as evident as Major Alden's rage when he went to see the latter, and asked for Mary. Mrs. Rodman happened to be in the house at the time, and what she didn't see she heard. She says the one thing you can't fool her about is a counterfeit gentleman. And Ralston Cary was no counterfeit."

"For Heaven's sake, don't get on what Mrs. Rodman thinks or says. Tell me about the marriage. I'm asking a lot of questions, but you're so slow."

"I'm telling as fast as I can. You interrupt so much with questions I can't finish." And Mrs. Moon's voice was real spunky.

"They were married in Washington," she began again. "The morning after the interview with the Major they caught the five-o'clock train, and that afternoon there was a telegram telling of the marriage.

"Her father never forgave Mary. Seven months later he died, and after settling up affairs there was nothing left. Alden House was mortgaged to the limit. There were a number of small debts as well as two or three large ones, and when these were paid and all accounts squared there was barely enough left for Parke to buy his railroad ticket to some city out West, where he had secured a place as resident physician in a hospital. That was thirteen years ago." She took a deep breath, as if thinking. "Thirteen years. Since then we've known little about him. You say he is a famous surgeon? We've never heard it in Yorkburg."

"Of course you haven't. Yorkburg has heard nothing since 1865. But there are a good many things it could hear." And Mrs. Grey laughed, but with her forehead wrinkled, as if she were trying to understand something that was puzzling her.

And then it was Mrs. Moon said something that made understanding come rolling right in on me. The answer to that look on Miss Katherine's face the night of the Reagans' ball was as plain as Jimmie Jenkins's nose, which is most all you see when you see Jimmie. It was like I thought. It was a man.

"Ophelia," said Mrs. Moon, and she moved her chair closer to Mrs. Grey, and leaned forward with her hands clasped, "did you ever hear Doctor Alden speak of a Miss Trent--Miss Katherine Trent?"

"No. You mean--"

"Yes; she's the one. Parke Alden and Katherine Trent were sweethearts from children. Shortly after Mary's marriage something happened. There was a misunderstanding of some kind, and they barely bowed when they met. Everybody was sorry, for it was one of the matches Heaven might have made without discredit. Soon after Parke went away, Katherine went off to some school just outside of Philadelphia, and, so far as is known, they've never seen each other since."

Mrs. Grey brought both hands down on her knees. "I knew it was something like that. I knew it! Doctor Alden is just that sort of a man. And it's Katherine Trent? I wish I'd known it before she went away."

"What would you have done?" Mrs. Moon looked frightened. She's very timid, Mrs. Moon is, and always afraid of telling something she oughtn't. "What could you have done?"

"Looked at her better. She's certainly good to look at. Not beautiful, but a face you never forget. And Doctor Alden is the kind that never forgets. But tell me something about the child. How did she get here?"

"Her nurse brought her. Her father kept her after her mother's death, taking her about from place to place with this old negro mammy until she was three, when he died suddenly, strange to say, in the same place his wife died, Mobile, Alabama."

"Why did the nurse bring her here? Was she a Yorkburg darkey?"

"No; but she had heard Mr. Cary say there was an Orphan Asylum here, and not knowing what else to do, she came on with her. She told the Board ladies she had heard the child's father say a hundred times he would rather see her dead than have her mother's family take her. And she begged them not to let it be known who she was until she was old enough to understand."

Just then Bobbie Moon laid out flat on his back and kicked up his heels. And Billie looked so disgusted, I stopped the story I was trying to tell.

"You ain't talking sense," he said. "And I'm not going to listen any more. An ant can't eat an elephant in half an hour and leave no scraps." And he rolled over and began to fight Bobbie.

Sarah Sue and Myrtle, who'd been playing with their mother's muff and tippet, got to fussing so about which should have her hat that Mrs. Moon, hearing it, jumped up, and I heard her say:

"Mercy me! Do you suppose she heard?"

I never was so glad of a fight in my life. The more fuss was made the more chance there was of my being forgot, and presently I told Mrs. Moon I had to go home. The boys said they didn't care, my stories were rotten anyhow, and out I went and ran so fast I had such a pain in my side I could hardly breathe.

But I didn't go in right away. I couldn't. Inside of me everything was thumping: "Mary Alden, your Mother; Mary Alden, your Mother; Mary Alden, your Mother." There was no other thought but that.

Presently I turned and went down to King Street, to where the Reagans live, and in the dark I stood there and shook my fist at my dead grandfather. I hated him for treating my mother so. Hated him! Then I burst out crying, and cried so awful my eyes were nearly washed out.

There were twelve and a half years' worth of tears that had to come out, and I let them come. After they were out I felt lighter.

But sleep? There wasn't a blink of it for me all night. I was so mixed up with new feelings that I was sick in my stomach, and my old conscience got so sanctimonious that if I could have spanked it I would.

I wasn't eavesdropping; I know that's nasty. But forty times I'd been punished for speaking when I shouldn't, and, besides, it was my duty to find myself. They saw me, and then forgot. If they hadn't wanted me to know what they were saying, they shouldn't have said it.

But that didn't do my conscience any good. I hate a conscience. It's always making you feel low down and disreputable. I don't believe I will say anything to my children about one, and let them have some peace.

For two days I didn't have any. Then I decided I'd wait until Miss Katherine came, and not say anything to her or to anybody about what I'd heard until I found out a little more about that remembrance in her face. But the waiting for her is the longest wait I've ever waited through yet.

It certainly is queer what a surprise you are to yourself. Before I knew that my mother and her father and his father and some other fathers behind him had lived in the Alden House, I would have given all I own, which isn't much, just my body, to have known it. And I guess I would have been that airy Martha couldn't have lived with me, and would have had to take Mary to the pump to bring her senses back with water. Mary is my best part, but at times she hasn't half the common sense she needs, and frequently has a pride Martha has to attend to.

But after I found out I had the same kind of blood in me that Mrs. General Rodman had in her, though I'm thankful it isn't mentioned on the family's tombstones, it didn't seem half as big a thing as I thought.

I was ashamed of the way it had acted, and of the way it had treated my father. He was too much of a gentleman to talk about his, whether high or low, and I know nothing about him. But I adore his memory! I am his child as well as Mary Alden's, and that's a thing my children are never going to forget. Never.

And now the part I'm thinking of most is what was said about Miss Katherine and Dr. Parke Alden being sweethearts when they were young. He has been away thirteen years, Mrs. Moon said, and Miss Katherine is now twenty-eight. I know she is, because she told me so.

Thirteen from twenty-eight leaves fifteen, so she was fifteen when they had that fuss and he went off. Fifteen was awful young to love hard and permanent; but Miss Webb says Miss Katherine was born grown and stubborn, and when she once takes a stand she keeps it.

I wonder what she took the stand with Uncle Parke for? She is right quick and outspoken at times, and I bet he made her mad about something.

But she ought to have known he was a man, and not expected much. I know my children's father is going to make me so hopping at times I could shake him. If he didn't, he would be terrible stupid to live with, and nothing wears you out like stupidness. I don't really mind a scrap. It's so nice to make up.

But I believe that's the reason Miss Katherine don't get married. Because in her secret heart Dr. Parke Alden is still her sweetheart. I know in his secret heart she is still his. She's bound to be if she ever once was.

Glorious superbness! Wouldn't that be grand? If they were to get married she would be my really, truly Aunt! The very thought makes me so full of thrills I can't sit still when it comes over me.

Oh, Mary Martha Cary, what a beautiful place this world could be!

XII
A TRUE MIRACLE

A secret isn't any pleasure. What's the use of knowing a thing you can't let anybody know you know? If I can't tell soon what I've heard about myself something is liable to happen.

Nearly three months have passed, and I haven't told yet. I'm still holding out, but it's the most awful experience I ever had.

Another idea has come to me, and if I could see Miss Katherine I could tell whether to do it or not. If she don't come soon I will do it, anyhow. I won't be able to help it.

The girls say if I were a darkey they'd think I was seeking. That's because some days I'm so unnatural quiet and stay so much by myself. I do that for safety, fearing otherwise I'd speak.

They don't know what's going on inside of me. If they could see they'd find nothing but quiverings and questions, and if I don't do anything really violent it's all I ask.

Every morning and every night my prayers are just this: "O Lord, help Mary Cary through this day. I'm not asking for to-morrow, it not being here yet. But *This Day* help me to hold out." And all day long I'm saying under my breath:

"Hold on, Mary Cary, hold on, hold on.
There never was a night that didn't have a dawn.
There never was a road that didn't have an end.
Wait awhile, wait awhile, and then the letter send."

I say that so often to myself that I'm afraid somebody will hear me think it. If that letter isn't sent soon, the answer will be received by a corpse.

I'm never again going to have a secret. It's worse than a tumor or dropsy. Mrs. Penick has a tumor. I've never seen the dropsy, but a secret is more dangerous, for it dries you up. Dropsy has water to it.

We had apple-dumplings for dinner. I sold mine to Lucy Pyle for two cents, and bought a stamp with it. The stamp is for The Letter.

Miss Katherine has come back. Came night before last, but I've been too excited to write anything down. Everything I do is done in dabs these days, and few lines at the time is all I'm equal to.

She looks grand. And oh, what a difference her being here makes! We are children, not just orphans, when she is with us; and it's because she loves us, trusts us, brings our best part to the top that we are different when she is about. The very way she laughs--so clear and hearty--makes you think things aren't so bad, and already they have picked up. Like my primrose does when I give it water, after forgetting it till it is as limp as old Miss Sarah Cone's crepe veil.

I haven't told her anything yet, but I've been watching good. I haven't seen any particular signs of memories and regrets, she being too busy to have them since she got back. Still, I believe they are there, and I'm that afraid I'll say Parke Alden in my sleep I put the covering over my head, for fear she'd hear me if I did.

I am back in her room, and this afternoon she asked me what I was looking at her so hard for. I told her she was the best thing to look at that came my way, and she laughed and called me a foolish child. But Mary Cary is thinking, and she isn't telling all she thinks about, either.

Well, it's written. That letter is written and gone. It was to Dr. Parke Alden. I sent it to his hospital in Michigan. I made it short, because by nature I write just endless, having gotten in the habit from making up stories for the girls and scribbling them off when kept in, which in the past was frequent. This is what I wrote:

DR. PARKE ALDEN:

Dear Sir,--Eleven weeks and two days ago I heard you did not know I was living. I am. I live in the Yorkburg Female Orphan Asylum, and have been living here for nine years and four months and almost a week. If you had known I was living all these years and had not made yourself acquainted with me, I would not now write you. But I heard, by accident, you did not know I had been born, so I am writing to tell you I was. It happened in Natchez, Miss. I know that much, but little more, except my father was an actor. I worship his memory. My mother was named Mary Alden, and you are her brother. If you would like to know more, and will write and ask me, I think you will learn something of interest. Not about me, but there are other people in this world.

Respectfully,

MARY CARY.

Three days have passed since I sent that letter off secret. I wouldn't let Miss Katherine know for a billion dollars that I'd sent it, but I'm glad I did. I'm sure she's got something in her heart she don't talk about, for last night, when she didn't know I was looking, I saw that same quiet proudness come in her face I saw the night of the ball.

I don't know how long it takes to go to Michigan, not knowing much about travelling, as I've never been out of Yorkburg since I came in. But some day I'm going around the world, and I'm going to see everything anybody else has ever seen before I marry my children's father. Of course, after I get married he will be busy, and there will be always some excuse that will make you tired. I'm going beforehand. Miss Webb says marriage is very uncertain.

This is a grand day. The crocuses are peeping up just as pert and pretty. The little brown buds on the trees have turned green and getting bigger every day, and even the air feels like it's had a bath. I just love the spring. Everything says to you: "Good-morning! Here we are again. Let's begin all over." And inside I say, "All right," and I mean it; but oh, Mary Cary, you're so unreliable. There are times when your future looks very much like a worm of the dust.

Miss Bray is real sick. She hasn't been well for a long time, and she looks like she's shrivelling, though still fat. She has nervous dyspepsia, which they say is ruinous to dispositions, and Miss Bray's isn't the kind for any sort of sickness to be free with.

It certainly is making her queer, for she's changed from sharpness to tearfulness, and she weeps any time. A thing I never thought I'd live to see.

Poor creature, I feel real sorry for her. Miss Jones says she's worn out, but I don't believe it's that. I believe it's conscience and coffee. Miss Bray isn't an all-over bad person. If it wasn't I knew she told stories, I could have stood the other things. But when a person tells stories, what have you got to hold on to? Nothing.

I believe it's those stories that's giving her trouble in her stomach. Anything on your mind does, and Miss Bray looks at me so curious and so nervous, sometimes, that I can't help feeling sorry for her.

I don't believe she will ever get well until she repents and confesses and crosses her heart that she won't do it again. A confession is a grand relief.

Suppose Dr. Parke Alden don't write, don't notice me! I will be that mad and mortified I will wish I was dead. But if he don't answer that letter, I will write a few more things to him before dying, for, if I am an Orphan, I oughtn't to be treated like a piece of imagination.

The black hen has got a lot of little chickens and the jonquils are in bloom. The sun is as warm as June, but I'm shivering all the time, and Miss Katherine says she don't understand me. She gave me a tonic to make me eat more. I don't want to eat. I want a letter.

*   *   *   *   *

Jerusalem the Golden! Now, what do you reckon has happened! Nothing will evermore surprise Mary Cary, mostly Martha.

If the moon ever burns, or the stars come to town, or the Pope marries a wife, or the dead come to life, I will just say, "Is that so?" and in my heart I will know a stranger thing than that.

Yesterday Miss Bray sent for me to come to her room. She was sick in bed, and her frizzes weren't frizzed, and she looked so old and pitiful that I took hold of her hand and said, "I'm awful sorry you are sick, Miss Bray."

And what did she do but begin to cry, and such a long crying I never saw anybody have. I knew there was a lot to come out and she'd better get rid of it, so I let it keep on without remarks, and after a while she told me to shut the door, and get her a clean handkerchief out of her top bureau-drawer.

I did it. Then she told me to sit down. I did that, too, and it's well I did. If I hadn't I'd have fell. Her words would have made me.

"Mary Cary," she said, "you have given me a great deal of trouble, and at times you've nearly worried me to death. But never since you've been here have you ever told a story, and that's what I've done." And she put her head down in her pillow, and I tell you she nearly shook herself, out of bed she cried so.

I was so surprised and confused I didn't know whether I was awake or asleep. But all of a sudden it came to me what she meant, and I put my arms around her neck and kissed her. That's what I did, Martha or no Martha; I kissed her. Then I said:

"Miss Bray, I'm awful glad you are sorry you did it. If you're sorry it's like a sponge that wipes it off, and don't anybody but you and me and God know about that particular one. And we can all forget it, if there's never any more."

And then she cried harder than ever. Regular rivers. I didn't know the top of your head could hold so much water.

But she said there would never be any more, for she'd never had any peace since the way I looked at her that day, and she couldn't stand it any longer. She didn't know why I had that effect on her, but I did, and she'd sent for me to talk about it.

Well, we talked. I told her I didn't think just being sorry was enough, and I asked her how sorry was she.

"I don't know," she said, and then she began on tears again, so I thought I'd better be quick while the feeling lasted.

"Well, you know, Miss Bray," I began, "Pinkie Moore hasn't been adopted yet. She never will be while the ladies think what you told them is true. You ought to write a letter to the Board and tell them what you said wasn't so."

"I can't!" she said; and then more fountains flowed. "I can't tell them I told a story!"

"But that's what you did," I said. "And when you've done a mean thing, there isn't but one way to undo it--own up and take what comes. But it's nothing to a conscience that's got you, and is never going to let you go until you do the square thing. If you want peace, it's the only way to get it."

"But I can't write a letter; I'm so nervous I couldn't compose a line." And you never would have known her voice. It was as quavery as old Doctor Fleury's, the Methodist preacher who's laid off from work.

"I'll write it for you." And I hopped for the things in her desk. "You can copy it when you feel better." And, don't you know, she let me do it! After three tryings I finished it, then read it out loud:

> DEAR LADIES,--If any one applies for Pinkie Moore, I hope you will
> let her go. Pinkie is the best and most useful girl in the Asylum.
> More than two years ago I said differently. It was wrong in me, and
> Pinkie isn't untruthful. She hasn't a bad temper, and never in her
> life took anything that didn't belong to her. I am sorry I said
> what I did. She don't know it and never will, and I hope you will
> forgive me for saying it.
>
> Respectfully,
>
> MOLLIE E. BRAY.

When I was through she cried still harder, and said she'd lose her place. She knew she would. I told her she wouldn't. I knew she wouldn't. And after a while she sat up in bed and copied it. Some of her tears blotted it, but I told her that didn't matter, and when I got up to go she looked better already.

I knew how she felt. Like I did when my tooth that had to come out was out. And a thing on your mind is worse than the toothache. One you can tell, the other you can't. A thing you can't tell is like a spook that's always behind you, and right in the bed with you when you wake up sudden, and lies down with you every time you go to sleep. I know, for that letter is on my mind.

When I got out of Miss Bray's room I ran in mine, Miss Katherine being out, and locked the door, and I said:

"Mary Martha Cary, don't ever say again there's no such things as modern miracles. There's been a miracle to-day, and you have seen it. Somebody has been born over." And then, because I couldn't help it, I cried almost as bad as Miss Bray.

But, oh, nobody can ever know how much harm it had done me to believe a lady could go through life telling stories, and doing mean, dishonorable things, and not minding. And people treating her just the same as if she were honest!

When I found out it wasn't so--that your sin did make you suffer, and that it did make a difference trying to do right--I felt some of my old Martha-ry scornfulness slipping away. And I got down on my knees, no words, but God understanding why.

I don't like any kind of bitterness in my heart. I'd rather like people. But can you like a deceiver? You can't.

Dr. Parke Alden has taken no more notice of me than if I were a Juney-bug.

I wonder if Miss Katherine will ever marry. She wasn't meant to live in an Orphan Asylum. She was meant to be the Lady of the House, and to wear beautiful clothes, and have horses and carriages and children of her own, and to give orders. Instead of that, she is here; but sometimes she has a look on her face which I call "Waiting." Last week I wrote a poem about it. This is it:

"In the winter, by the fireside, when the snow falls soft and white,
I am waiting, hoping, longing, but for what I don't know quite.
And when summer's sunshine shimmers, and the birds sing clear and sweet,
I am waiting, always waiting, for the joy I hope to meet.

It will be, I think, my husband, and the home he'll make for me;
But of his coming or home-making, I as yet no signs do see.
But I still shall keep on waiting, for I know it's true as fate,
When you really, truly hustle, things will come if just you'll wait."

I don't think much of that. It sounds like "Dearest Willie, thou hast left us, and thy loss we deeply feel." But I wasn't meant for a poet any more than Miss Katherine for an old maid.

Dr. Parke Alden must be dead. Either that or he's no gentleman, or he didn't get my letter. I wish I hadn't written it. I wish I hadn't let him know I was living.

But it was Miss Katherine I was thinking about. Thank Heaven, I didn't mention her name! He isn't worth thinking about, and I think of nothing else.

XIII
HIS COMING

I f I could get out on the roof and shake hands with the stars, or dance with the man in the moon, I might be able to write it down; but everything in me is bubbling and singing so, I can't keep still to write. But I'm bound to put down that he's come. He's come!

He came day before yesterday morning about ten o'clock. I was in the school-room, and Mrs. Blamire opened the door and looked in. "Mary Cary can go to the parlor," she said. "Some one wishes to see her."

I got up and went out, not dreaming who it was, as I was only looking for a letter; and there, standing by a window with his back to me, was a man, and in a minute I knew.

I couldn't move, and I couldn't speak, and Lot's wife wasn't any stiller than I was.

But he heard me come in, and turned, and, oh! it is so strange how right at once you know some things. And the thing I knew was it was all true. That he'd never known about me until he got my letter. For a minute he just looked at me. We didn't either of us say a word, and then he came toward me and held out his hands.

"Mary Cary," he said. And the first thing I knew I was crying fit to break my heart, with my arms around his neck, and he holding me tight in his. His eyes were wet, too. They were. I saw them. He kissed me about fifty times--though maybe not more than twenty--and I had such a strange feeling I didn't know whether I was in my body or not. It was the first time that any one who was really truly my own had ever come to see me since I'd been an Orphan, and every bit of sense I ever had rolled away like the Red Sea waters. Rolled right away.

I don't remember what happened next. Everything is a jumble of so many kinds of joys that I've been crazy all day. But I wasn't too crazy to see the look on his face, I mean on my Uncle Dr. Parke Alden's face, when he saw Miss Katherine coming across the front yard. We were standing by the window, and as he saw her he looked again, as if he didn't see good, and then his face got as white as whitewash. He took out his handkerchief and wiped his lips and his forehead that were real perspiring, and I almost danced for joy, for I knew in his secret, secret heart she was his sweetheart still. But I didn't move even a toe. I just said:

"That's Miss Katherine Trent. She's the trained nurse here. Did you know her when she lived in Yorkburg?"

And he said yes, he knew her. Just that, and nothing else. But I knew, and for fear I'd tell him I knew, I flew out of the room like I was having a fit, and met Miss Katherine coming in the front door.

"Miss Katherine," I said, "there's a friend of yours in the parlor who wants to see you. Will you go in?"

She walked in, just as natural, humming a little tune, and I walked behind her, for I wanted to see it. I will never be as ready for glory as I was that minute. I could have folded my hands and sailed up, but I didn't sail. It's well I didn't, for they didn't meet at all like I expected, and I was so surprised I just said, "Well, sir!" and sat right down on the floor and looked up at them.

They didn't see me. They didn't see anything but each other; but if they'd had the smallpox they couldn't have kept farther apart, just bowing formal, and not even offering to shake hands.

My, I was set on! I didn't think they'd meet that way; but Miss Becky Cole, who's kinder crazy, says God Almighty don't know what a woman is going to do or when she's going to do it. Miss Katherine proved it. She didn't fool me, though, with all her quietness and coolness. I knew her heart was beating as hard as mine, and I jumped up and said:

"I think you all have been waiting long enough to make up, and it's no use wasting any more time." And I flew out, slamming the door tight, and shut them in.

I don't know what happened after I shut that door. But, oh, he's grand! He is thirty-six, and big and splendid. He and Miss Katherine are in the parlor now. Miss Jones says everybody in Yorkburg knows he's here, and all talking. All!

I've been so excited since the first day he came that I've had little sense. But my natural little is coming back, and I'm trying not to talk too much. Of course, I had to say a good deal, because everybody had to know how it happened that Doctor Alden came back to Yorkburg so suddenly after thirteen years' being away. And why he hadn't been before, and what he came for and when he was going away, and if he were going to take me with him.

And then everybody remembered how he and Miss Katherine used to be sweethearts when they were young. I tell you, the talking that's been going on in Yorkburg in the last few days would fill a barrel of books. By the end of the week a whole lot more will be known about Uncle Parke than he knows about himself. If Yorkburg had a coat of arms it ought to be a question-mark.

They've had time to talk over everything that ever happened since Adam and Eve left Paradise, in the long walks they take, and in the evenings when he calls, which he does as regular as night comes. And now I'm waiting for the news. I'll have to be so surprised. And I guess I will be. Love does very surprising things.

Miss Katherine knew where Uncle Parke was all the time. She knew who I was, too; that is, she found out after she nursed me at the hospital. But what that fuss was about I don't know. Nothing much, I reckon; but the more you love a person the madder you can get with them. And from foolishness they've wasted years and years of together-ness.

But it's all explained now, and I don't think there's going to be any more nonsense. They are going to be married as sure as my name isn't in a bank-book; and if signs are anything, it's going to be soon.

Miss Bray is better, though she looks pretty bad still. She's been awfully excited about Uncle Parke's coming, and she says she hears he's very distinguished and real rich. Isn't it strange how quick some people hear about riches? I don't know anything of his having any. He hasn't mentioned money to me; but oh, I feel so safe with him! He's so strong and quiet and easy in his manners, and he's been so splendid and beautiful to me. He don't use many words. Just makes you understand.

I wonder what a man says to a lady when he wants her to marry him? I know Dr. Parke Alden isn't the kind to get down on his knees. If he were, Miss Katherine would certainly tell him to get up and say what he had to say standing, or sitting, if it took long. But I'll never know what he said. They're not the kind to tell; but they can't hide Love. It's just like the sun. It can't help shining.

*   *   *   *   *

Land of Nippon, I'm excited! I believe he's said it!

The reason I think so is, I saw them late yesterday evening coming in from a long walk down the Calverton road, where there's a beautiful place for courters. When they got to the gate they stopped and talked and talked. Then he walked to the door with her, still holding his hat in his hand, and though it was dark I could feel something different. I was so nervous you would have thought I was the one.

I was over by the lilacs; but they didn't see me. I didn't like to move. It might have been ruinous, so I held my breath and waited.

When they got to the door they stopped again, and presently he held out his hand to say good-bye. The way he did it, the way he looked at her made me just know, and I got right down on my knees under the lilac-bush, and when he'd gone I sang, "Praise God, from whom all blessings flow." Sang it loud.

I didn't care who heard. I wasn't telling why I was thankful. Just telling I was. Oh, Mary Martha Cary, to think of her being your really, truly Aunt! The very next thing to a mother!

XIV
THE HURT OF HAPPINESS

I wouldn't like to put on paper how I feel to-day. Uncle Parke has gone. Gone back to Michigan. I'm such a mixture of feelings that I don't know which I've got the most of, gladness or sadness or happiness or miserableness, and I'd rather cry as much as I want than have as much ice-cream as I could hold.

But I'm not going to cry. I don't like cryers, and, besides, I haven't a place to do it in private. I wouldn't let Miss Katherine see me, not if I died of choking. I ought to be rejoicing, and I am; but the female heart is beyond understanding, Miss Becky Cole says, and it is. Mine is. I could die of thankfulness, but I'd like first to cry as much as I could if I let go.

They are engaged. Uncle Parke and Miss Katherine are, and they are to be married on the twenty-seventh of June. That's my birthday. I will be thirteen on the twenty-seventh of June.

They told me about it night before last. I was out on the porch, and Miss Katherine called me and told me she and Doctor Alden wanted me to go to walk with them. I knew what was coming. Knew in a flash. But I pretended not to, and thanked her ever so much, and told her I'd just love to go.

We walked on down to the Calverton road, talking about nothing, and making out it was our usual night walk, but when we got to the seven maples Uncle Parke stopped.

"Suppose we sit down," he said. "It's too warm to walk far to-night." And after we sat he threw his hat on the ground, then leaned over and took my hands in his.

"Mary Cary," he began. And though his eyes were smiling, his voice was real quivering. I was noticing, and it was. "Mary Cary, Katherine and I have brought you with us to-night to ask if you have any objection to our being married. We would like to do so as soon as possible--if you do not object."

He turned my face to his, and the look in his eyes was grand. It meant no matter who objected, marry her he would; but it was a way to tell me--the way he was asking, and I understood.

"It depends," I said, and, as I am always playing parts to myself, right on the spot I was a chaperon lady. "It depends on whether you love enough. Do you?"

"I do. For myself I am entirely sure. As to Katherine--Suppose she tells you what she thinks."

I turned toward her. "Do you, Miss Katherine? It takes--I guess it takes a lot of love to stand marriage. Do you think you have enough?"

In the moonlight her face changed like her opal ring when the cream becomes pink and the pink red.

"I think there is," she said. Then: "Oh, Mary Cary, why are you such a strange, strange child?" And she threw her arms around me and kissed me twenty times.

After a while, after we'd talked and talked, and they'd told me things and I'd told them things, I said I'd consent.

"But if the love ever gives out, I'm not going to stay with you," I said. "I'm never going to be fashionable and not care for love. A home without it is hell."

"Mercy, Mary!" Uncle Parke jumped. "Don't use such strong language. It isn't nice."

"But it's true. I read it in a book, and I've watched the Rices. When there's love enough you can stand anything. When there isn't, you can stand nothing. Living together every day you find out a lot you didn't know, and love can't keep still. It's got to grow or die."

Then I jumped up. "I always could talk a lot about things I didn't understand," I said. "But I consent." And I flew down the road and left them.

I've written it out on a piece of paper, about their being engaged, and looked at it by night and by day since they told me about it. I've said it low, and I've said it loud, but I can't realize it, and the little sense the Lord gave me He has taken away.

They say I did it. Say I'm responsible for every bit of it, and that I will have to look after them all the rest of their lives to see that I didn't make a mistake in writing that letter. And that I'm to go to Europe with them on their wedding tour and live with them always and always. And--oh!--I believe my heart is going to burst with miserable happiness and happy miserableness, and my head feels like it's in a bag.

Dr. Parke Alden and Miss Katherine Trent are the two nicest people on earth, and the two I love best. But I don't think they know all the time what they are doing and saying. They are that in love they don't see but one side--the happy side-- and they think I am going to leave this place with a skip and a jump and run along by them, third person, single number, and not know I'm in the way.

They won't even listen when I tell them I don't know what I'm going to do. I know what I want to do! Everything in me gets into shivering trembleness when I think I could go to Europe with them on their wedding trip. Think of it! Mary Cary could go to E-U-R-O-P-E!

They've invited me and say I'm to go, because I'm never to leave them any more, and they want me. But it isn't so. Mary tries to believe it's so, but Martha knows it isn't. They think they think they want me, but they don't; nobody wants an outsider on a wedding tour, and I'm not going. I can't help it. Come on, tears! Even angels sometimes cry aloud; and, not being a step-relation to one, I'm going to let Mary cry if she wants to. Sometimes Martha is real hard on Mary.

There is no use studying Human Nature. You can't study a thing that changes by day and by night, and is so uncertain you never know what it is going to do. Now, here is Mary Cary, mostly Martha, who would rather get on a train or a boat and go somewhere--she don't care where--than to do any other thing on earth. Who has never seen anything and wants to see everything, and who, if anyone had told her a year ago she could go to New York, and then to Europe, would have slid down every flight of stairs head foremost from pure joy. And now she has the chance, she is not going. She is Not.

She hasn't much sense, Mary Cary hasn't, but enough to know wedding trips are personal, and, besides, the girls have turned into regular weepers. Every time anything is said about going away their eyes water up, and Martha feels like a yellow dog with no tail. I know they hate Miss Katherine's going; but why do they cry about my going? Lord, this is a strange place to live in, this world is! I wonder what heaven will be like?

Miss Bray is much better. She says Uncle Parke has cured her. I don't believe it. I believe it was Relief of the Mind.

*   *   *   *   *

I wasn't meant to be a sad person. I was silly sad the other day; but I've found out when anything bothers you very much, it helps to take it out and look at it. Walk all around it, poke it and see if it's sure enough, and, if it isn't, tell it you'll see it dead before you'll let it do you that way.

That's what I did with what was making me doleful, and now I'm all right again. It was because I did want to go to Europe awful, and it twisted my heart like a machine had it when I turned my back on the chance. And then, too, it was because the girls begged me so not to go away for good that I got so worried.

They said it wouldn't be the same if I wasn't here, and though they didn't blame me, they begged me so not to go that I got as addled as the old black hen that hatched ducks.

Now, did you ever hear of such a thing? As if it really mattered where Mary Cary lived! I didn't know anybody truly cared, and finding out made me light in the head. But I know that's just passing--their caring, I mean. I'm much obliged; but they'll forget it in a little while, and I will be just a memory.

I hope it will be bright. There's so much dark you can't help that a brightness is real enjoyable. They say what you look for you see, and what you want to forget you mustn't remember. There are a lot of things about my Orphan life I'm going to try to forget. But there are some that for the sake of sense, and in case of airs, I had better bear in mind. I guess Martha will see to those. Whenever Mary gives signs of soaring, Martha brings her straight back to earth. Martha doesn't care for soarers, and she has a terrible bad habit of letting them know she don't.

Yorkburg hasn't settled down yet, and is still hanging on to the last remnants of the surprise about Uncle Parke's coming, and about his marriage to Miss Katherine and my going away.

Of course, Miss Amelia Cokeland wanted to know if he'd made the Asylum a present, and how much. At first nobody would tell her. She's got such a ripping curiosity that there isn't a sneeze sneezed in Yorkburg, or a cake baked, or a door shut that she doesn't want to know why. But maybe she can't help it. Some people are natural inquirers, and that's the way she makes her living, telling the news.

She used to work buttonholes, but since she can't see good she just spends the day out and tells all she hears. Nobody really likes her, but her tongue is too sharp to fool with. To keep from being talked about, everybody pretends to be friendly.

I don't. She shook her finger at me once because I wouldn't tell her what was in Miss Katherine's letter the first time she went away, and since then she's never noticed me until Uncle Parke came. Now every time I see her she's awful pleasant, and tries to make me talk. But a finger once shook is shook. I don't talk.

But Uncle Parke did make the Asylum a present. He didn't tell me, neither did Miss Katherine, and I don't think he wanted anybody but the Board ladies to know. But, of course, they couldn't keep it secret. They told their husbands, and that meant the town. Nothing but a dead man could keep from talking about money.

It must have been a lot he gave, for Peelie Duke told me she heard Mrs. Carr and Mrs. Dent talking about it the day she took some apple-jelly for Miss Jones over to little Jessie Carr, who was sick.

"He could have kept her at a fashionable boarding-school from the day she was born until now for the sum he's turned over to the Board," said Mrs. Carr, and her eyes, which are the beaming kind, just danced, Peelie said.

"Well, he ought to," grunted Mrs. Dent, who talks like her tongue was down her throat. "He ought to! We've been taking care of the child for almost ten years. I hear he wants the house put in good condition, a new dining-room and kitchen built and four bath-rooms. The rest is to go to the endowment. I think more ought to go to the endowment and less for these luxuries. I don't approve of them. An Orphan Asylum is not a hotel."

"No, but it ought to be a home, if possible," said Mrs. Carr, and Peelie said she looked at Mrs. Dent like she wondered how under heaven her husband stood her all the time.

I certainly am glad to know I'm paid for. Some day, when I'm grown and earning my own living, before I marry my children's father, I am going to give as much as I can of that money back to Uncle Parke. Of course that will be some time off, and until then I'll just have to try to be a nice person.

Miss Katherine says a whole lot of people would pay a big price to have a nice person in the house with them--one of those cheerful, sunshiny kind that helps and is encouraging, and gets up again when they fall down. As I can't earn money yet,

I'm going to try to be something like that, so they won't be sorry I ever was born. Uncle Parke and Miss Katherine won't.

But isn't it strange, when the time comes for you to do a thing you are crazy to do, you wish it hadn't come?

There have been days when I hated this Asylum. I've felt at times that I was just one of the numbers of the multiplication table, and in all my life I'd never be anything else. And I'd almost sweep the bricks up out of the yard, I'd be so mad to think I was nothing and nobody.

I wanted to be something and somebody. I didn't want to die and be forgotten. I would have liked to sit on St. John's Church steeple and have everybody look at me and say:

"That's Mary Cary! She's great and rich, and gives away lots of money and sings like an angel." That's what I once would have liked, but I've learned a few things since I didn't know then.

One is that high places are lonely and hard and uncomfortable, and people who have sat on them have sometimes wished they didn't. Miss Katherine told me that herself, also that the place you're in is pretty near what you're fitted to fill. Otherwise you'd get out and fill another.

I've given up steeples and superiorities. But I'm glad I'm not going to be an orphan, just an orphan, all my life. I'm glad; still, when I think of going away and leaving everybody and everything: the old pump, where I drowned my first little chicken washing it; and the old mulberry-tree, where my first doll was buried; and the garret, where I made up ghost-stories for the girls on rainy days; and the school-room; and even No. 4--when I think of these things, I could be like that man in the Bible (I believe it was David, but it might have been Jonah), I could lift up my voice and weep.

But I'm not going to. Weepers are a nuisance.

I guess that's the way with life, though. When things are going, you try to hold them back. And if you got them, you'd maybe wish you hadn't.

That's the way Mrs. Gaines did when her husband died. I mean when he didn't die that first time. She thought he was going to, and so did everybody else. He had Fright's disease, and it affected his heart, being liable to take him off any time, and Mrs. Gaines just carried on terrible.

She had faintings and hysterics, and said she couldn't live without him, though everybody in Yorkburg knew she could, and easy enough. He without her, too, had she gone first. She had asthma and an outbreaking temper, and he drank.

Mrs. Mosby--she's the doctor's wife--said she didn't blame him. No man could stand Mrs. Gaines all the time without something to help, and everybody hoped when he got so ill that he'd die and have a little rest. But he didn't. He got better.

Mrs. Gaines was so surprised she was downright disagreeable about it, and how he stood it was a wonder. He didn't long, for the next summer he was dead sure enough, and Mrs. Gaines put on the longest crepe veil ever seen in the South, she said. It touched the hem of her skirt in front and behind; but she cut it in half after everybody had seen it often enough to know how long it was.

If Augustus Gaines thought she was going to ruin her eyes and choke her lungs by wearing unhealthy crepe over her face he thought wrong, she said, and in a few months it was gone and she was as gay as a girl. She's what they call a character, Mrs. Gaines is.

I don't want to be like her, and I don't expect to do any groaning over leaving Yorkburg. I want to live with Uncle Parke and Miss Katherine, and I'm going to. But it's strange how many happy things hurt.

XV
A REAL WEDDING

It looks as if everybody who knows Miss Katherine wants her to be married from their house. Her brothers want her to be married from theirs. Her aunt, Mrs. Powhatan Bloodgood, who lives in Loudon County, and whose husband is as rich as a real lord, begs her to be married in hers; and everybody in Yorkburg--I mean the coat-of-arms everybodies--has invited her to have the wedding in their home.

But she just smiles and says no to them all. Says she is going to be married from her house, which is the Orphan Asylum, though the ceremony will be at the church. It's going to be in the morning at twelve o'clock, so they can take the two-o'clock train for Richmond and go on to New York.

Miss Katherine wants it to be quiet, but it can't be quiet. There's nothing on human legs that can use them who won't be at the church to see that wedding take place.

Everybody has been paying her a lot of attention of late. It's real strange what a difference a man makes in a marriage, even if he isn't noticed much in person at the time. If he's rich and prominent, everybody is so pleasant and sociable you'd think they were real intimate. If he's just good and poor, few take notice.

When Miss Vickie Toones married Mr. Joe Blake they didn't get hardly any presents. They had a lot of dead relations who used to be rich and haughty, but their living ones are as poor as the people they didn't used to know, and hardly anybody gave them anything handsome.

Miss Katherine's presents are just amazing, and my eyes are blistered by the shine of them. I didn't know before such things were in the world. People say Uncle Parke has made a lot of money in some mines out West, besides being a doctor, and that he doesn't have to work. "But a man who doesn't work hasn't any excuse for living," I heard him tell somebody, and maybe it's so, though I don't know.

I don't know anything these days. I'm the shape and size of Mary Cary, but I see and hear so many things I never saw and heard before that I'd like to borrow a dog to see if he knows whether I am myself or somebody else. And another thing I'd like to find out is, How do other people know so much?

Mrs. Philip Creekmore has a cousin whose wife's brother lives in the same place Uncle Parke does, and Miss Amelia Cokeland wrote out there and found out all about him. But it doesn't matter whether she truly knows anything or not. Miss Webb says she is like those fish scientists. Give her one bone, and she can tell you all the rest. She's had a grand time telling more things about Uncle Parke than Miss Katherine will ever learn in this world.

My dress is finished. I'm to be Maiden of Honor. There are no bridesmaids. Think of it! Me, Mary Cary, once just flesh and blood mechanical, now a living creature who is to wear a white Swiss dress and a sash with pink rosebuds on it, and walk up the church aisle with my arms full of roses. And--magnificent gloriousness! most beautiful of all!--every girl in this Asylum is to have a white dress and a sash the color she likes best to wear to the wedding. That's my wedding gift to the girls. Uncle Parke gave it to me.

Miss Katherine's California brother and his wife have come. I don't like them. He looks bored to death, and chews the end of his mustache till you wonder there's any left. As for her, she's the limit. Maybe that's what's the matter with him.

She seems to be afraid some of us might touch her, and she stares as if we were figures in a china-shop. No more says good-morning than if we were.

She wears seven rings on one hand and four on another, and rustles so when she walks she sounds like a churner out of order. If she isn't a bulgarian born, she's bought herself into being one, for she oozes money. It's the only thing you think of when she's around. You can actually smell it. I think Miss Katherine is sorry they came. She don't say it, of course, but plenty of things don't have to be said.

Uncle Parke came last night, bringing his best friend and some others. The best one is Doctor Willwood. He's fine. He and I are going to come down the aisle together. I reach up to his elbow, and he says he may put me in his pocket. I wish he would. I know I will be that frightened I'd be glad to get in it.

He wants to know all about Yorkburg and the people, and to-day Miss Bray let me take him all around the town and show him the antiquities. He asked her. I had on the white dress Miss Katherine gave me last summer, and I looked real nice, for I had on my company manners, too.

You see, he was from the West, and had never been to Virginia before; and when a man comes such a long way, one ought to put on company manners and be extra polite. It wouldn't be right not to. I put mine on, and I guess I did do a lot of talking. I'm by nature a talker, just like I can't help skipping when my heart is happy and nothing hurts.

I told him about all the places we came to, and about who lived in them, except the Alden house which the Reagans now possess. When we got there he stopped in front of it.

"My!" he said, "that's a beautiful old place! Whose is it?"

"Some people by the name of Reagan live there," I said. "I don't know them." And I started on.

I came near forgetting, and saying, "That is Alden house, where my grandfather used to live," but I remembered in time. I don't acknowledge my grandfather, and I knew somebody else would tell him Uncle Parke was born and lived there until he went West.

We had a grand time. We stayed out over four hours, and I forgot all about dinner. He didn't want to go in when I suddenly remembered and told him I must, and then he said I was going to take dinner with him at the Colonial. He'd asked Miss Bray, and it was all right. And that's what I did. Took dinner with him at the Colonial!

I tell you, Mary Martha Cary had what you could truly call a Time. And Doctor Willwood said he never had enjoyed a morning in his life like that one. Laugh? I never heard a man laugh so hearty. Half the time I couldn't tell why. I'd be real serious, but he'd look at me and almost die laughing. I bet I said some things I oughtn't, but I don't remember, and I couldn't take them back if I did.

*   *   *   *   *

It's over. The wedding is over. Everything is after a while in this life, even death; and time is the only thing that keeps on just the same.

They're gone. Gone on their bridal tour, and the happiness that's left Yorkburg would run a family for a long life. I wish everybody could have seen that wedding. It's going to be long remembered, for the earth and sky, and birds and flowers, and trees and sunshine all took part. Everything tried to help, and as for blessings on them, they took away enough for the human race. But now it's over I feel like my first balloon looked when I stuck a pin in it to see what would happen. I saw.

I had a telegram from them to-day. It said:

We sail at eleven o'clock. Love to all, and hearts full for Mary Cary.

UNCLE PARKE and AUNT KATHERINE.

Well, she's my Aunt now. That's fixed, anyhow, and the marriage that fixed it was a beauty. Every bird in Yorkburg was singing, every flower was blooming, and every heart was blessing; and when those fifty-eight orphans walked in, all in white and two by two, every hand was dropping roses. And that is what each girl was wishing: Roses, roses all her life!

After the ushers, I came in all alone by myself; that is, my shape did. Mary was really inside the altar looking at me coming up slow and easy, and Martha was ordering me to keep step to the music. "All right, I'm doing my best," I was saying to both. And I was, but I was thankful when I got to where I could stop, for my legs were so excited I wouldn't have been surprised if they'd turned and run out.

Behind me came Miss Katherine, on her Army brother's arm. He's as nice as the other isn't. He hasn't got the money-making disease. When Uncle Parke and Doctor Willwood came out of the vestry-room Uncle Parke gave me one look, just one, but it was so understanding I winked back, and then he came farther down and stood by Miss Katherine like she was his until kingdom come, forever more. Amen.

Then the minister began, and the music was so soft you could hear the birds outside. The breeze through the window blew right on Miss Katherine's veil, and I was so busy watching it I didn't know the time had come to pray, and I hardly got my head bent before I had to take it up again. Then the minister was through, and I was walking down the aisle with Doctor Willwood, and in just about two minutes more we were back at the Asylum, and it was all over--the thing we'd been looking forward to so long.

The Asylum looked real nice that morning. There were bushels and bushels of flowers in it, for everybody in town who had any sent them. Flowers cover a multitude of poverties. The reception was grand. That California Richness called it a breakfast, but that was pure style. Yorkburg don't have breakfast between twelve and one, and everybody else called it a reception. As for the people at it, there were more kinds than were ever in one dining-room before; and every single one had a good time. Every one.

You see, Miss Katherine, besides being who she was, was what she was. Having known a great deal about all sorts of people since being a nurse, and finding out that the plain and the fancy, the rich and the poor, those who've had a chance and those who haven't, are a heap more alike than people think, she said she was going to invite to her wedding whoever she wanted. And she did.

There wasn't one invited who didn't come: the bent and the broke and the blind (that's true, for old Mr. Forbes is bent, and Mrs. Rowe's hip was broken and she uses crutches, and Bobbie Anderson is blind); and the old, that's the high-born coat-of-arms kind; and the new, that's the Reagans and Hinchmans and some others, and Mr. Pinkert the shoemaker, who, she says, is a gentleman if he don't remember his grandfather's name; and Miss Ginnie Grant, who made her underclothes--all were there. All. It was a different wedding from any that was ever before in Yorkburg, and if any feelings were hurt it was because they were trying to be. Some feelings are kept for that purpose.

Of course, Mrs. Christopher Pryor had remarks to make. "Katherine always was too independent," I heard her tell Miss Queechy Spence. "But I don't believe in anything of the kind. If you once let people get out of the place they were born in, there'll be no doing anything with them. You mark me, if this wedding don't make trouble. Some of these people will expect to be invited to my house next." And she took another helping of salad that was enough for three. She's an awful eater.

"Oh no, they won't," said Miss Queechy. "They know better than to expect anything like that of you," and she gave me a little wink and walked off with Mr. Morris, who's her beau. I went off, too. It isn't safe for Martha Cary to be too near Mrs. Pryor, for Mary never knows what she may do.

And, oh, you ought to have seen Miss Bray! She was stepsister to the Queen of Sheba. Solomon never had a wife arrayed like she was on that twenty-seventh day of June. I believe she is engaged to Doctor Rudd. I really do.

You see, after people got over teasing him about that make-believe wedding, he got to thinking about her. He's bound to know he isn't much of a man, and no young girl would have him, so lately he's been ambling 'round Miss Bray. If he can stand her, he'll do well to get her. She's a grand manager on little.

He was at the wedding, too. His beard was flowinger and redder, and the part in the back of his head shininger than ever. He had an elegant time. He was so full of himself you would have thought it was his own party.

Uncle Parke and Aunt Katherine have been on the ocean three days. I wonder if they are sick. I don't think I will go to Europe with my children's father. I was seasick once on land, and there wasn't a human being I even liked that day. It would be bad to find out so soon that the very sight of your husband makes you ill. After you know him better, you could tell him to go off somewhere; but at first I suppose you have to be polite.

They were awful nice about wanting me to go with them. The bride and groom were. They said I had to, and they were so surprised when I said I couldn't that they didn't think I meant it. When they found out I did, they were dreadfully worried, and didn't know what to do next. There wasn't anything to do, and here I am. Here I'm going to be, too, until the first day of October, when they will be back, and we will start for the West, for Michigan.

I'm going to like Michigan. I've decided before I get there. I know there will be something to like, there always is in every place and every person, Miss Katherine says, if you just will see it instead of the all wrong. I was by nature born critical. There are a lot of things I don't like in this world, but there's no use in mentioning them. As for opinions, if they're not pleasant they'd better be kept to yourself. I learned that early in life and forget it every day.

I'm going to try and think Michigan is a grand place, and next to Virginia the best to live in. They couldn't, ***couldn't*** expect me to think it was like Virginia!

Perhaps, after a while, Uncle Parke may come back. For over two hundred years his people have lived here, and sometimes I believe he feels just like that dog did who had his call in him. The call of the place that the first dogs came from, that wild, free place, and I think Uncle Parke wants to come back, wants to be with his own people.

Out West is very convenient, though, Peggy Green says. She has an aunt who used to live out there, and she told her you could do as you choose in almost everything. If husbands and wives didn't like each other, there was no trouble in getting new ones. They could get a divorce and marry somebody else.

I wonder what a divorce is. We've never had one in Yorkburg, and I never knew until the other day that when you got married it wasn't really truly permanent. I thought it was for ever and ever and until death parted. The prayer-book says so, and I thought it meant it.

By the time I'm grown I guess I'll find a lot of things are said and not meant. Maybe when I find out I will be all the gladder to come back to Yorkburg, where people don't seem to know much about these new-fashioned things. Where they still believe in the old ones, and just live on and don't hurry, and are kind and polite and dear, if they are slow and queer and proud a little bit.

It makes me have such a funny feeling in my throat when I think about going away. I'm trying not to think. But I do. Think all the time. I want this summer to be the happiest the children ever had. It's the last for me. That sounds consumptive, but I don't mean that way. I mean it's my last Orphan summer.

Of course, I'm glad, awful glad; but I'm so sorry the other children aren't going, too. For them it's prunes and blue-and-white calico to look forward to until they're eighteen. Year in and year out, prunes and calico.

But maybe it isn't. If Mary Cary will do her part something nicer may happen. She doesn't know yet the way to make it happen, having nothing much to send back but love. Somebody says love finds the way. Oh, Mary Cary, you and Love ***must*** find a way!

The Codes Of Hammurabi And Moses
W. W. Davies

QTY

The discovery of the Hammurabi Code is one of the greatest achievements of archaeology, and is of paramount interest, not only to the student of the Bible, but also to all those interested in ancient history...

Religion   **ISBN:** *1-59462-338-4*   **Pages:**132
MSRP $12.95

The Theory of Moral Sentiments
Adam Smith

QTY

This work from 1749. contains original theories of conscience amd moral judgment and it is the foundation for systemof morals.

Philosophy   ISBN: *1-59462-777-0*   **Pages:**536
MSRP $19.95

Jessica's First Prayer
Hesba Stretton

QTY

In a screened and secluded corner of one of the many railway-bridges which span the streets of London there could be seen a few years ago, from five o'clock every morning until half past eight, a tidily set-out coffee-stall, consisting of a trestle and board, upon which stood two large tin cans, with a small fire of charcoal burning under each so as to keep the coffee boiling during the early hours of the morning when the work-people were thronging into the city on their way to their daily toil...

Pages:84

Childrens   ISBN: *1-59462-373-2*   *MSRP $9.95*

My Life and Work
Henry Ford

QTY

Henry Ford revolutionized the world with his implementation of mass production for the Model T automobile. Gain valuable business insight into his life and work with his own auto-biography... "We have only started on our development of our country we have not as yet, with all our talk of wonderful progress, done more than scratch the surface. The progress has been wonderful enough but..."

Pages:300

Biographies/   ISBN: *1-59462-198-5*   *MSRP $21.95*

The Art of Cross-Examination
Francis Wellman

QTY

I presume it is the experience of every author, after his first book is published upon an important subject, to be almost overwhelmed with a wealth of ideas and illustrations which could readily have been included in his book, and which to his own mind, at least, seem to make a second edition inevitable. Such certainly was the case with me; and when the first edition had reached its sixth impression in five months, I rejoiced to learn that it seemed to my publishers that the book had met with a sufficiently favorable reception to justify a second and considerably enlarged edition. ..

Pages:412

Reference   **ISBN: *1-59462-647-2***   *MSRP $19.95*

On the Duty of Civil Disobedience
Henry David Thoreau

QTY

Thoreau wrote his famous essay, On the Duty of Civil Disobedience, as a protest against an unjust but popular war and the immoral but popular institution of slave-owning. He did more than write—he declined to pay his taxes, and was hauled off to gaol in consequence. Who can say how much this refusal of his hastened the end of the war and of slavery ?

Law   **ISBN: *1-59462-747-9***   **Pages:48**
MSRP $7.45

Dream Psychology Psychoanalysis for Beginners
Sigmund Freud

QTY

Sigmund Freud, born Sigismund Schlomo Freud (May 6, 1856 - September 23, 1939), was a Jewish-Austrian neurologist and psychiatrist who co-founded the psychoanalytic school of psychology. Freud is best known for his theories of the unconscious mind, especially involving the mechanism of repression; his redefinition of sexual desire as mobile and directed towards a wide variety of objects; and his therapeutic techniques, especially his understanding of transference in the therapeutic relationship and the presumed value of dreams as sources of insight into unconscious desires.

Pages:196

Psychology   **ISBN: *1-59462-905-6***   *MSRP $15.45*

The Miracle of Right Thought
Orison Swett Marden

QTY

Believe with all of your heart that you will do what you were made to do. When the mind has once formed the habit of holding cheerful, happy, prosperous pictures, it will not be easy to form the opposite habit. It does not matter how improbable or how far away this realization may see, or how dark the prospects may be, if we visualize them as best we can, as vividly as possible, hold tenaciously to them and vigorously struggle to attain them, they will gradually become actualized, realized in the life. But a desire, a longing without endeavor, a yearning abandoned or held indifferently will vanish without realization.

Pages:360

Self Help   **ISBN: *1-59462-644-8***   *MSRP $25.45*

QTY

The Rosicrucian Cosmo-Conception Mystic Christianity *by Max Heindel*   ISBN: *1-59462-188-8* **$38.95**
The Rosicrucian Cosmo-conception is not dogmatic, neither does it appeal to any other authority than the reason of the student. It is: not controversial, but is: sent forth in the, hope that it may help to clear...   *New Age/Religion Pages 646*

Abandonment To Divine Providence *by Jean-Pierre de Caussade*   ISBN: *1-59462-228-0* **$25.95**
"The Rev. Jean Pierre de Caussade was one of the most remarkable spiritual writers of the Society of Jesus in France in the 18th Century. His death took place at Toulouse in 1751. His works have gone through many editions and have been republished...   *Inspirational/Religion Pages 400*

Mental Chemistry *by Charles Haanel*   ISBN: *1-59462-192-6* **$23.95**
Mental Chemistry allows the change of material conditions by combining and appropriately utilizing the power of the mind. Much like applied chemistry creates something new and unique out of careful combinations of chemicals the mastery of mental chemistry...   *New Age Pages 354*

The Letters of Robert Browning and Elizabeth Barret Barrett 1845-1846 vol II   ISBN: *1-59462-193-4* **$35.95**
by Robert Browning and Elizabeth Barrett   *Biographies Pages 596*

Gleanings In Genesis (volume I) *by Arthur W. Pink*   ISBN: *1-59462-130-6* **$27.45**
Appropriately has Genesis been termed "the seed plot of the Bible" for in it we have, in germ form, almost all of the great doctrines which are afterwards fully developed in the books of Scripture which follow...   *Religion/Inspirational Pages 420*

The Master Key *by L. W. de Laurence*   ISBN: *1-59462-001-6* **$30.95**
In no branch of human knowledge has there been a more lively increase of the spirit of research during the past few years than in the study of Psychology, Concentration and Mental Discipline. The requests for authentic lessons in Thought Control, Mental Discipline and...   *New Age/Business Pages 422*

The Lesser Key Of Solomon Goetia *by L. W. de Laurence*   ISBN: *1-59462-092-X* **$9.95**
This translation of the first book of the "Lemegton" which is now for the first time made accessible to students of Talismanic Magic was done, after careful collation and edition, from numerous Ancient Manuscripts in Hebrew, Latin, and French...   *New Age/Occult Pages 92*

Rubaiyat Of Omar Khayyam *by Edward Fitzgerald*   ISBN:*1-59462-332-5* **$13.95**
Edward Fitzgerald, whom the world has already learned, in spite of his own efforts to remain within the shadow of anonymity, to look upon as one of the rarest poets of the century, was born at Bredfield, in Suffolk, on the 31st of March, 1809. He was the third son of John Purcell...   *Music Pages 172*

Ancient Law *by Henry Maine*   ISBN: *1-59462-128-4* **$29.95**
The chief object of the following pages is to indicate some of the earliest ideas of mankind, as they are reflected in Ancient Law, and to point out the relation of those ideas to modern thought.   *Religiom/History Pages 452*

Far-Away Stories *by William J. Locke*   ISBN: *1-59462-129-2* **$19.45**
"Good wine needs no bush, but a collection of mixed vintages does. And this book is just such a collection. Some of the stories I do not want to remain buried for ever in the museum files of dead magazine-numbers an author's not unpardonable vanity..."   *Fiction Pages 272*

Life of David Crockett *by David Crockett*   ISBN: *1-59462-250-7* **$27.45**
"Colonel David Crockett was one of the most remarkable men of the times in which he lived. Born in humble life, but gifted with a strong will, an indomitable courage, and unremitting perseverance...   *Biographies/New Age Pages 424*

Lip-Reading *by Edward Nitchie*   ISBN: *1-59462-206-X* **$25.95**
Edward B. Nitchie, founder of the New York School for the Hard of Hearing, now the Nitchie School of Lip-Reading, Inc, wrote "LIP-READING Principles and Practice". The development and perfecting of this meritorious work on lip-reading was an undertaking...   *How-to Pages 400*

A Handbook of Suggestive Therapeutics, Applied Hypnotism, Psychic Science   ISBN: *1-59462-214-0* **$24.95**
by Henry Munro   *Health/New Age/Health/Self-help Pages 376*

A Doll's House: and Two Other Plays *by Henrik Ibsen*   ISBN: *1-59462-112-8* **$19.95**
Henrik Ibsen created this classic when in revolutionary 1848 Rome. Introducing some striking concepts in playwriting for the realist genre, this play has been studied the world over.   *Fiction/Classics/Plays 308*

The Light of Asia *by sir Edwin Arnold*   ISBN: *1-59462-204-3* **$13.95**
In this poetic masterpiece, Edwin Arnold describes the life and teachings of Buddha. The man who was to become known as Buddha to the world was born as Prince Gautama of India but he rejected the worldly riches and abandoned the reigns of power when...   *Religion/History/Biographies Pages 170*

The Complete Works of Guy de Maupassant *by Guy de Maupassant*   ISBN: *1-59462-157-8* **$16.95**
"For days and days, nights and nights, I had dreamed of that first kiss which was to consecrate our engagement, and I knew not on what spot I should put my lips..."   *Fiction/Classics Pages 240*

The Art of Cross-Examination *by Francis L. Wellman*   ISBN: *1-59462-309-0* **$26.95**
Written by a renowned trial lawyer, Wellman imparts his experience and uses case studies to explain how to use psychology to extract desired information through questioning.   *How-to/Science/Reference Pages 408*

Answered or Unanswered? *by Louisa Vaughan*   ISBN: *1-59462-248-5* **$10.95**
Miracles of Faith in China   *Religion Pages 112*

The Edinburgh Lectures on Mental Science (1909) *by Thomas*   ISBN: *1-59462-008-3* **$11.95**
This book contains the substance of a course of lectures recently given by the writer in the Queen Street Hall, Edinburgh. Its purpose is to indicate the Natural Principles governing the relation between Mental Action and Material Conditions...   *New Age/Psychology Pages 148*

Ayesha *by H. Rider Haggard*   ISBN: *1-59462-301-5* **$24.95**
Verily and indeed it is the unexpected that happens! Probably if there was one person upon the earth from whom the Editor of this, and of a certain previous history, did not expect to hear again...   *Classics Pages 380*

Ayala's Angel *by Anthony Trollope*   ISBN: *1-59462-352-X* **$29.95**
The two girls were both pretty, but Lucy who was twenty-one who supposed to be simple and comparatively unattractive, whereas Ayala was credited, as her Bombwhat romantic name might show, with poetic charm and a taste for romance. Ayala when her father died was nineteen...   *Fiction Pages 484*

The American Commonwealth *by James Bryce*   ISBN: *1-59462-286-8* **$34.45**
An interpretation of American democratic political theory. It examines politica! mechanics and society from the perspective of Scotsman James Bryce   *Politics Pages 572*

Stories of the Pilgrims *by Margaret P. Pumphrey*   ISBN: *1-59462-116-0* **$17.95**
This book explores pilgrims religious oppression in England as well as their escape to Holland and eventual crossing to America on the Mayflower, and their early days in New England...   *History Pages 268*

www.bookjungle.com *email: sales@bookjungle.com fax: 630-214-0564 mail: Book Jungle PO Box 2226 Champaign, IL 61825*

QTY

The Fasting Cure by *Sinclair Upton* ISBN: *1-59462-222-1* **$13.95**
In the Cosmopolitan Magazine for May, 1910, and in the Contemporary Review (London) for April, 1910, I published an article dealing with my experi-ences in fasting. I have written a great many magazine articles, but never one which attracted so much attention... New Age/Self Help/Health Pages 164

Hebrew Astrology by *Sepharial* ISBN: *1-59462-308-2* **$13.45**
In these days of advanced thinking it is a matter of common observation that we have left many of the old landmarks behind and that we are now pressing forward to greater heights and to a wider horizon than that which represented the mind-content of our progenitors... Astrology Pages 144

Thought Vibration or The Law of Attraction in the Thought World ISBN: *1-59462-127-6* **$12.95**

by *William Walker Atkinson* Psychology/Religion Pages 144

Optimism by *Helen Keller* ISBN: *1-59462-108-X* **$15.95**
Helen Keller was blind, deaf, and mute since 19 months old, yet famously learned how to overcome these handicaps, communicate with the world, and spread her lectures promoting optimism. An inspiring read for everyone... Biographies/Inspirational Pages 84

Sara Crewe by *Frances Burnett* ISBN: *1-59462-360-0* **$9.45**
In the first place, Miss Minchin lived in London. Her home was a large, dull, tall one, in a large, dull square, where all the houses were alike, and all the sparrows were alike, and where all the door-knockers made the same heavy sound... Childrens/Classic Pages 88

The Autobiography of Benjamin Franklin by *Benjamin Franklin* ISBN: *1-59462-135-7* **$24.95**
The Autobiography of Benjamin Franklin has probably been more extensively read than any other American historical work, and no other book of its kind has had such ups and downs of fortune. Franklin lived for many years in England, where he was agent... Biographies/History Pages 332

Name	
Email	
Telephone	
Address	
City, State ZIP	

☐ **Credit Card**   ☐ **Check / Money Order**

Credit Card Number	
Expiration Date	
Signature	

Please Mail to: Book Jungle
PO Box 2226
Champaign, IL 61825
or Fax to: 630-214-0564

ORDERING INFORMATION
web*: www.bookjungle.com*
email*: sales@bookjungle.com*
fax*: 630-214-0564*
mail*: Book Jungle PO Box 2226 Champaign, IL 61825*
or PayPal *to sales@bookjungle.com*

Please contact us for bulk discounts

DIRECT-ORDER TERMS

**20% Discount if You Order
Two or More Books**
Free Domestic Shipping!
Accepted: Master Card, Visa,
Discover, American Express

www.ingramcontent.com/pod-product-compliance
Lightning Source LLC
Chambersburg PA
CBHW082016170626
46817CB00009B/3110